The

Tornado

Wranglers

Weather Jacked

Book 1

Sloane Fennimore

Hello. This is Sloane. I hope you enjoy reading book 1 of The Tornado Wranglers.

If you know someone who may enjoy it, please recommend it to them. Visit my website sloanefennimore.com anytime.

I would like to thank Heavenly Father above for His unchanging & unconditional love in good & in bad times.

Thank you also to my F.A.T.E. who always encourages me who loves our Heavenly Father like I do.

The Tornado Wranglers Weather Jacked

Lying face down in the dirt and grass, she could taste the earth. Foreign debris was stuck in her teeth covering her tongue. She began spitting and coughing to clear her mouth. Her clothing was soaking wet from the rain. The sky began lighting back up as the sun peeked through the clouds. She squinted as she looked carefully around. She managed to push herself up with her hands coming to her knees. Something was protruding from her ankle. What was it? It was impossible to stand up. It intensified the pain every time. The object in her ankle was some type of thin sheet metal. It was possibly four inches in length and an inch in width. The metal definitely lodged in the bone. Pulling it out wasn't a good idea.

Something wet was running down the side of her neck. It wasn't coming from her neck though. The cell phone she carried deep in her front jean pocket would allow her to check her neck. Its screen could be used as a mirror by recognizing her voice when saying the words cell mirror into the microphone on the front. It was much faster than taking a photo of herself which is something she rarely did. In 2165, social media no longer existed. Her mirror revealed little cuts on her face. One cut on her hairline below her right ear was causing tiny streams of blood to run down her neck. Glass may have been the culprit.

There were no signs of any cars. Her car must have been picked up by the tornado. She remembered seeing the tornado, slamming on her brakes, pushing open her car door against the high winds then running as fast as she could to jump into a ditch. The sound of the tornado was almost deafening. It was like standing next to a high speed freight train.

Hoping some cell towers had survived the tornado, she slowly dialed 911. Her ears had a high pitched ringing sound in them.

The female dispatcher's voice sounded like it was at the end of a long tunnel, "911, what is your emergency?"

Charlotte shouted, "I can barely hear you, I'm hurt. I got away from a tornado. I can't walk. I don't see my car anywhere. I don't see any other cars either."

The dispatcher spoke loud and clear to Charlotte, "Did you sign up for the cell pinging program through the 911 system this year? It can help us locate you if enough cell towers survived in that area."

Charlotte yelled into the phone not realizing she was yelling, "No. I never sign up for that. All I know is the last time I was on the road, I was on Road 450."

"Okay. I understand. Most people don't sign up. The road address will help us get to you. Do you feel you have any life threatening injuries?"

"No, I have metal sticking out of my ankle. I have cuts on my head and face. Besides that, I don't know."

"Remain calm. We will get someone to you as quickly as we can. We believe the storms are over for now."

"I don't think I can stand on my knees anymore."

"Can you see what is around you?"

"There are some torn up electric fences. The biggest thing near me is a giant white oak tree."

"Will you be able to get back up on your knees when you hear the ambulance?"

"Maybe."

"That might help us find you."

"How long do you think it will be?"

"It depends on how much debris the ambulance has to drive through on the way there. I can stay on the line with you until they get there."

"Okay. Thanks."

Charlotte was relieved to be talking with someone while she waited for help. "I'm just glad I got away from that thing. How powerful was it?"

"They think it was an F3 or an F4," said the dispatcher.

"I believe it. I'm happy to be alive!" Charlotte yelled.

"Maybe one day there won't be any tornadoes."

"That would be a dream come true," Charlotte said.

"It's too bad they can't wrangle them all."

"I know. We never know how many will hit at one time."
Charlotte tried standing on her knees again, "Um. I'm kind of
dizzy. The whole world is kind of movi…" Down Charlotte went.
She was face down again on the earth.

"Miss? Miss? Are you still there?" The phone hit the
ground. The dispatcher couldn't hear anything. The dispatcher
looked at one of her coworkers, "I think she just passed out."
Sirens were wailing as they searched for Charlotte. Jeremy was
driving the ambulance.

"Dispatch said she just passed out," Jeremy shouted to the
back. "It's going to be hard to see her with all of this debris
everywhere. There's someone's rooftop flipped upside down over
there. We know she's near a big white oak tree. You don't see
many oaks in this area. Somehow it survived this mess."

The ambulance was slowly moving through all of the
debris.

"I hope we find her soon. There's no telling how long
she's been out here. There's the oak tree, but I don't see her,"
Jeremy said.

Kirsten was in the back of the ambulance, "I have the
thermal camera on." A mast had risen out of the top of the
ambulance. It was searching the area as the ambulance moved.
Kirsten was looking at the images as they popped up on the back
windows. "There are a couple of squirrels. I see some wild turkeys
moving around on the ground. I see her now. Let's stop." The

images disappeared from the windows as Kirsten jumped out of the back of the ambulance. She knelt down next to Charlotte who was still face down in the dirt.

Jeremy backed up the ambulance a little more to get closer. He grabbed the stretcher to take it over to Charlotte. They slowly rolled Charlotte onto her back then placed her on the stretcher. Charlotte had a pulse, was still breathing, but wasn't conscious.

"Let's try out this new tech stretcher," said Jeremy. He pushed a button on the side of the stretcher. The stretcher strapped Charlotte to itself. It levitated then parked itself inside the ambulance.

Charlotte was dreaming on the stretcher. She could see the giant tornado coming right at her car. It was hard to not be entranced by it. Time seemed to almost stop as the tornado whipped things up from the ground. The hail was pounding her car. She grabbed a clipboard from the passenger seat to cover her head as she jumped out racing toward what she believed to be a ditch. The softball sized hail was coming down so hard; it broke the plastic clipboard into a few pieces. As she jumped she tried to make her body as flat as possible, a loud oomph escaped from her mouth. Charlotte screamed out trying to lift her head while on the stretcher.

Kirsten was rubbing Charlotte's arm. "It's okay. We're going to get you to the hospital. You passed out after you called for help. You are in an ambulance. You are safe."

Charlotte groaned, "For a minute I thought I was back on the ground again. I hate tornadoes."

Kirsten smiled down at Charlotte, "We all do. Looks like you're going to survive it. Thankfully. There's an awful lot of property damage. It's taking a while to drive through it all even with the special tires we use on the ambulance, but we'll get you there. Let me ask you a few questions on the way. What is your name?"

"Charlotte Coles."

"Do you know what day it is?"

"Yes. It's Thursday."

"Do you know what month it is?"

"November."

"No, but that's okay. It's actually August."

"Now, tell me the year."

"2165."

"Let's test your vision."

"How many fingers am I holding up?"

"Two."

"Which two?"

"Your index and middle finger."

Jeremy called to the back, "We're almost there ladies. It's just a couple more minutes."

"Thanks Jeremy," said Kirsten.

The Tornado Wranglers Weather Jacked

The hospital was underground. The previous hospital that was built above ground had been totally destroyed twenty years before. They managed to get as many people as they could into the basement before the tornado hit, but it was one of the strongest the area had seen. When they decided to rebuild, they thought underground would be best. At the time, no technology had existed to fight a tornado. Scientists around the world were working on it, but couldn't figure out how to make it safe to use outside of a laboratory environment. Some people began building their houses underground due to the storms. It didn't take long for others to catch on that it was the safest thing to do. Sometimes people would build a dome home above and partially below ground. The dome shape stood up better to high winds.

A group of medical staff suddenly surrounded Charlotte. Many hands were grabbing at her, hooking her to things, looking her over, and asking her questions. These doctors had treated thousands of storm victims over the years, so they knew what to look for. The metal protruding from her ankle seemed to be the biggest issue. One doctor had his face right upon the area with a light atop his head. "It looks like this will need surgery," the doctor commented. "It's quite deep in your ankle. You were given Morphine for the pain. Since you're not screaming, I take it you can't feel it?"

"No, I never felt it." Charlotte was bleary-eyed. She waved her hand back as if dismissing the question.

"Your body's adrenaline kicked in protecting you from the pain. A surgeon will be in soon."

"Okay," Charlotte closed her eyes and began dreaming again. This time she dreamt that she didn't need to run from the tornado. Seth was there. He was standing firm, facing the storm. Just as he cradled the weapon in his arms and aimed it at the storm, Charlotte awoke to a clanging sound. Her heart was racing as her eyes searched her room. One of her visitors had accidentally bumped a metal flowerpot. It was lying on the floor.

"I told you not to stand so close to that!" growled Charlotte's mom.

"It's okay Dad," mumbled Charlotte.

Her parents were so happy to see she was talking. Her dad stood up as he was cleaning up the mess on the floor, "These rooms aren't very roomy."

"How are you feeling?" asked Charlotte's mom.

"They must still be giving me morphine, so not bad," she giggled. Her parents both smiled. "How many tornadoes did they get?"

"Three," her dad answered.

"Let me guess, Seth and his team were at every one of them."

"You're right." Her dad answered.

Charlotte smiled, "If only they could clone that guy and his team. Seth could have wrangled my tornado too. Then we could have had a beer after."

"Since when do you drink beer?" Charlotte's mom asked.

"I would drink one with him. I hate the taste, but I wouldn't mind," Charlotte said.

Charlotte's mom walked over taking Charlotte's hand into her own, "Seth is a great hero and so is his team. He's also pretty rough honey. I don't think he's your type."

"Mom, I know you mean well. I would like to find out for myself someday what he is really like. You can't tell who a person is from a few news stories. Those are just tiny little snippets of their life. It doesn't represent them as the whole person. Especially with all of the editing that's done for ratings," Charlotte rolled her eyes.

"Do you know how many girls are after him?" asked Charlotte's mom.

"Yes I do. I think I have just as good of a chance as any of them." Charlotte answered.

Charlotte's dad spoke up, "Just remember, he makes a living risking his life. That's something that affects not only him, but anyone who is closest to him as well."

"I'll be careful Dad."

Charlotte's dad gave her a quick kiss at the top of her forehead, "We better get out of here for a while so you can rest."

"Sounds good. I'll be dreaming about Seth." Charlotte giggled. She closed her eyes and began to rest.

Storm Warriors

Seth was six foot one, dark complexion, dark hair, dark brown eyes, dark long eyelashes, and muscular. He worked out daily lifting weights. Seth was like the front man of a band. The other wranglers were at the storms too, but they stayed behind in the vehicle working the computers that sent data to his weapon. This kept them safe from the weapon. If anything went wrong, only one person would suffer the consequence instead of the whole team. It took a human touch to operate the gun. Robots were not trusted with the technology due to deadly consequences suffered in the past.

The vehicles they used were called Tornado Seeker Vehicles or TSVs for short. The team did not view themselves as heroes even though the public frequently hailed them as such. If it weren't for them, much more death and destruction would exist. Seth's team called themselves, *The Tornado Wranglers.*

The weapon Seth used was The Rankoweitz Laser Plasma Accelerator Gun named after the last scientist that got it working outside the laboratory without causing any deaths. Eight other scientists worldwide died while testing it over several years before

The Tornado Wranglers Weather Jacked

Rankoweitz who lived in Poland figured out exactly what was necessary to make it safe. He had only suffered a hand injury involving the gun. His middle finger, ring finger, and pinky finger on his right hand had gotten melded together during a test shooting. The beam splitter Rankoweitz came up with seemed to be one of the keys to the safety of the gun. Since the name of the gun was such a mouthful, the team of wranglers nicknamed it the Hydra. Rankoweitz was known worldwide as a hero for his amazing work.

All of *The Tornado Wranglers* were meteorologists, but chasing storms and wrangling them was their passion to save as many lives as possible. They wanted to save property too. People were still warned about tornadoes because wranglers could not reach every one of them. Doppler radar was the best way to find a tornado, but gut feelings also led them to the tornadoes they wrangled.

There were teams all over the country, but Seth's team in particular was the best. Working out in the gym three hours a day was common for the team. It was important they were all in good shape in case anyone would ever have to fill in for Seth. They had two TSVs. One was for backup. Both TSVs could withstand high winds of up to 300 miles per hour due to their dome shape. Each TSV had radar with computers inside. It was important for them to have a 360 degree view so there was shatterproof glass wrapped around each vehicle with chairs that swiveled 360 degrees so they could always see in any direction. The unpredictable nature of these storms warranted this.

Other storm chasers who did not have wrangling ability in years past had been killed. They were caught in storms that developed so quickly they weren't seen on radar. They didn't survive once the vehicle was slammed back into the earth. Some technology was developed that would allow the vehicles to bounce if falling to the ground once picked up unexpectedly. *The Tornado Wranglers* had just invested some of their money into this technology. They had one TSV equipped with it.

Technology was expensive, so four times a year, storm chasers across the nation would do fund raising events. Rain wrapped tornadoes were the worst. New technology allowed them to see these on a computer screen even if it was pitch black outside. The data could be sent to eyeglasses, so the man wrangling could also see the tornado. Both of *The Tornado Wranglers'* vehicles had this special technology as well.

No matter how much technology was available, it was still a life and death situation especially if equipment failed for some reason. Paramedics would volunteer their time to go along in case any medical assistance was needed for the wranglers or for people caught in the storms. Various cameras were attached to each TSV to study the footage later. The footage was used on newscasts as well in an attempt to keep people from venturing out into the

The Tornado Wranglers Weather Jacked

tornadoes. For whatever reason, tornadoes seemed to almost hypnotize people leading them to their death.

It was workout time at headquarters. Seth was lifting weights while lying on his back. He had a dumbbell in each hand. He was counting to twenty for each set. Each day when he worked out, he thought about the last time he saw his mother. The memory for him was always so vivid. He could see his mother struggling with the large door that had lain flat on the floor to the basement's opening. It was heavy making it hard to pull up to flip open. The stairs were steep that led to a dirt floor. The storm was so loud, Seth's mother was shouting as loudly as she could as she pushed Seth forward, "Go, go, go," she yelled. "It's right on top of us…" Seth fell to the dirt floor. As he turned back to look for his mother, he caught a glimpse of her being flipped through the sky. She had tried to hold onto the house. The suction from the tornado was too strong. She was screaming Seth's name as the tornado pulled her legs first into the sky.

The basement door slammed shut. It was dark. A musty smell was in the air. There was very little light coming through the basement windows. Dirt had covered the windows from the storm. Seth was only ten at the time. He wondered if somehow, some way, maybe his mom had made it through. He called out for her several times hoping she was just outside the basement door. He heard nothing in return. He kept yelling even though there was nothing but the sounds of sprinkling rain. Eventually his yells became whimpering cries that turned into hiccupping. His face was wet with tears. The collar of his shirt was soaked with tears as it stuck to his neck. He would have vomited had he anything in his stomach. He felt numb as tears continued to stream down the sides of his face.

He looked around trying to remember what his mother had told him when they had gotten through other storms. How he wished he had paid more attention to what she had said. He knew somewhere in the basement there were some flashlights, a radio, blankets, pillows, and food. It was so dark now that he wasn't sure if he would be able to search for these things. It was so much easier when his mom guided him to these things. They would sit to wait for everything to blow over.

He crawled along the dirt floor feeling his way to the corner of the basement. If he remembered right, there was a small room there. He thought that room might be where he and his mom had gone before. He bumped his head on something hard. It was a large trunk. He remembered his mom getting the flashlights from the trunk. He felt around and found a flashlight. He went to turn it on, but nothing happened. He tried it again. It still didn't work. He felt around the trunk again to find another flashlight. He turned it on, but the light was really dim. He shined it into the trunk. There was a giant pack of batteries in a hard plastic container that was snapped shut. He quickly unsnapped the plastic container. Being alone in the dark made him nervous. Seth decided to use the dim light to load the other flashlight with new batteries. That did the trick. It was really bright in there now.

He found the radio next to the batteries in the trunk. The radio had a crank on it, so no batteries were necessary. After cranking the handle several times to wind it up, it came on. He remembered how his mother had done that several times in the past. It was already turned on the local weather radio setting. The announcer was stating that there were many trees down, cars overturned, buildings destroyed, and several deaths. The announcer then gave the all clear, which meant it was over now. People could call for help to assess damages.

When Seth was growing up there were lots of people who did not take the weather warnings seriously. Many people died because of it. His mother always took it seriously. Sometimes he would go to school to hear kids talking about how they didn't do anything when the sirens went off. The sirens meant that a tornado had been spotted and to take cover. He had a couple of classmates that had their homes destroyed. They had ended up in the hospital with several injuries.

Seth was thinking about those kids. He hoped they had lived through this one. He didn't think his mom had. There were two telephones in the basement. One was a land line. The other was an emergency satellite phone in case the land line was down. The land line was definitely down. There was no dial tone. It was totally dead. He remembered his mom showed him there was a special place to stand in the basement when using the satellite phone. He walked around a bit with the satellite phone trying different areas of the basement. He finally got a dial tone. He dialed 911.

Jess was standing over Seth at the weight bench, "Hey Seth, you finished with these weights now?"

Seth snapped out of the memory, "Yeah. Go ahead, Jess. I'm going to hit the shower now."

Jess started counting out loud as Seth walked away. Jess liked working out. It gave him energy that helped him focus. Jess started with *The Tornado Wranglers* when Seth started. Jess was muscular too. He had blonde hair that he kept really short. His eyes were dark blue. He was six feet tall. He liked to keep his body hair to a minimum. He had one those devices that people see advertised on television that he used frequently to get rid of his body hair. After repeated use, the hair doesn't grow back at all. Jess liked that. Seth poked fun at him quite often because of it.

Just like Seth, Jess had bad memories of storms from his childhood too. As Jess worked out, his mind flashed back to when he was twelve, he and his parents went shopping as they often did. They were in a giant discount store looking for clothes. Jess was constantly growing out of his clothing. It was the weekend. The store was packed full of people. They knew there was a tornado watch going on, but most people didn't take watches very seriously back then. A watch meant that conditions were favorable for a tornado to form. People would just go about their normal routine as if there was nothing to worry about.

As the people inside were oblivious to the situation, the sky went from sunny to gray. The winds started whipping up violently. Discarded items such as plastic cups, plastic bags, and aluminum cans along the roadside were being tossed into the air. Some items were staying in the air then swirling into the sky. The birds stopped singing. The tornado sirens began whining. The shoppers inside could clearly hear it. Some people ignored it as if nothing was happening. Others were quietly walking around looking for the best place to hide. Most people knew that the sirens meant a tornado had been spotted nearby and to take cover.

A loud whistling sound came over the intercom system in the store then a woman's scratchy voice, "Attention shoppers. A tornado has been sighted. The State Weather Service estimates ten minutes to take cover. There is no basement here. The safest places here are in our restrooms and walk–in coolers. We cannot keep you here against your will, but if you leave, it may not be safe to drive."

Jess knew what to do when he was home during a storm. He wasn't quite sure what they were going do in this big store. Jess's parents stayed calm. His dad started heading toward the coolers at the back of the store.

A store employee was waving to people to come on back, "We have a few giant coolers back here folks. Come on back."

Jess and his parents made it safely to the coolers. The employee got as many people as he could inside all of the coolers.

Jess always got a little nervous when he knew a tornado might be on its way. It was pretty chilly inside the cooler even with other people standing around. His dad tried to comfort him, "Don't worry Jess. We probably won't be in here long. The tornado may miss us altogether." Jess nodded to his dad as he stared at the cooler's cement floor.

Suddenly, there was a huge bang then the lights flickered. Jess's mom took hold of his hand. He nestled up to her the best he could while they stood there unsure of what would happen next. The tornado sirens began whining again. There was such a hush in the cooler, he wondered if anyone was breathing. Then came the loudest screech. People began screaming throughout the store. The lights began blinking off then blinking on, blinking off then blinking on again.

Jess closed his eyes. He felt his dad's arms envelope he and his mother. Hail came down in buckets. It sounded like ball bearings hitting the metal roof. Suddenly, there was silence then WHOOSH. It sounded like a wooden roller coaster at top speed flying by. There was a loud suction sound like the sound water makes as it quickly gets sucked down a drain. It was as if a giant vacuum was trying to sweep up the store. The sound turned to silence. Everything went dark. A few seconds later some emergency lights came on.

The Tornado Wranglers Weather Jacked

A store employee who had been listening to a scanner knew it was safe now, "Okay everyone, we made it through." He opened the cooler door.

Jess and his parents were behind a group of about ten people. They could hear them gasping as they walked. Debris was everywhere. It literally looked like a war zone inside the store. Part of the roof had been ripped off. Everywhere Jess looked, there were people crying or just sitting on the floor gazing around in shock. One man was sitting under a tipped over clothing rack. His head was bleeding. Jess's dad walked up to the man. He asked the man if he needed help. The man did not answer, so Jess's dad knelt down right in front of him. He looked the man in the face and asked if he was okay. The man was in his late 70's. The man gave Jess's dad his hand to help him up off of the floor.

The man started yelling, "I can't hear anything. My hearing aids don't work half of the time. I didn't know the storm was coming. I saw people moving quickly. I didn't understand what was happening. Thanks for helping me up. My name is Olson."

Jess's dad introduced himself, "No problem, I'm Henry. This is my wife Lila, and my son Jess. Let's take a look at the cut on your head." Henry looked at the cut. It didn't seem like anything that needed immediate assistance. "Olson, are you dizzy at all, did you bump your head?"

"No, I don't think I bumped it. I think one of those hangers scratched it open. Thanks again. I should go see if my truck survived this storm. I need to head back home." Olson was stepping over things trying to find his way to the parking lot.

"I think he'll be okay. Let's look around to make sure that there isn't anyone else who needs our help," said Henry. By that time there were several emergency crews on site. Most people had made it to an area where they were protected, so didn't suffer any major injuries. Henry, Jess, and Lila were slowly finding their way out of the store. They would stop from time to time asking people if they needed anything.

Jess found himself almost tripping over someone's arm. Henry pulled Jess back as he was about to fall, "Whoa, I've got you." Henry bent down to touch the arm. It felt lifeless. He could see the rest of the woman's body had many wet clothes piled over top of it. Lila stood back as Jess and Henry began digging through the clothing to get to her, "Faster Jess, we need to get to her." The woman was outstretched. She did not look alive. Her light blue eyes were wide open. Henry knelt beside her to check for a pulse, "Jess, get a paramedic. Now!"

Henry straddled the woman. He put his hands on her chest. Henry felt the crunch under his hands with the first compression he gave the woman. He did not stop until the paramedics came to his assistance. The woman was still staring at the ceiling. The paramedics shocked her several times to try to get her heart started, but to no avail. They worked on her for several minutes before giving up. Jess couldn't help but watch when the woman's body would jolt up with each shock. He was talking to himself inside of his head wanting the lady to live. He buried his head in his dad's side when the paramedics gave up. Right then and there is when Jess decided he was going to chase storms when he grew up.

Meeting Heroes

Charlotte woke up in her hospital bed. She turned on the news to watch the weather. The hospital planned to release her the next day. It would take her ankle a while to completely heal from the surgery. The footage on TV was amazing as always. The camera on a TSV had caught footage of Seth preparing to defeat a tornado. You could hear his crew speaking with one another and speaking with him.

Seth was suited up. He had on body armor that was really lightweight so that he could be out of the way quickly if he needed to be. In order to defeat a tornado, he had to pay really close attention to the team leader who kept a close eye on which direction the tornado would be heading. Even though they had lots of technology helping them track tornadoes, the storms were still unpredictable. Jess was directing Seth.

They didn't have to be right on top of the tornado for the technology to work. They could be up to a quarter of a mile away. Visibility was always poor, so Seth used special glasses designed to see rain wrapped tornadoes which were invisible to naked eyes. The glasses connected with the Doppler radar that is used to track the storms. The camera work made it seem like they were right on top of the tornado. Someone inside the dome vehicle had control of the cameras. They could zoom in or out to take video or still pictures.

There was Seth standing with a wide stance. His armor was designed to protect Seth against flying objects. He couldn't just stand there and let things fly off of him like a superhero in the movies, but he usually came out of it with just some bruises from flying debris. He wore tight fitting black leather pants with a tight fitting black long sleeved shirt underneath the armor. The armor itself was a shiny metallic color made from a material similar to Kevlar which was custom fitted snugly around his muscular legs, arms, chest, and stomach. It was thin and flexible, but super strong like metal. His helmet was tight and metallic looking. He always wore the special glasses which wrapped around his head. The lenses of the glasses were mirrored. This particular tornado he was trying to wrangle was moving at what seemed like a slower speed than what Seth was used to. He felt like he had time to aim the Hydra slowly.

The Tornado Wranglers Weather Jacked

The Hydra was lightweight, but didn't look it. It took both hands to hold it. When it was fired, it had a little kick to it. It had a large wide barrel that he would slide one hand underneath then with his other hand he had to pull a trigger to make it shoot. The barrel was about a foot and a half in length. The total weight of the Hydra was around ten pounds. It was fusion powered with power cells that snapped into the butt of the gun. Those were also developed by Rankoweitz who was a complete genius! Rankoweitz got the idea from auto makers who started selling fusion powered cars back in the twenty first century.

Seth relied on his team to program the gun with how far it would shoot and how long the gun would stay on to wrangle the tornado. Seth's goal was to aim where the team told him to aim and hold it there as tightly as possible. If something went wrong with communication between the computers and the Hydra, Seth had the option to manually wrangle the tornado using manual programming on the gun itself which may not be as precise as the information coming from the computers. This rarely happened, but was a good back-up instead of just abandoning the mission.

Jess let Seth know that they should be able to see the tornado coming in about five seconds. Seth locked himself in place preparing for more wind. The boots he wore had large hidden spikes he could turn on with a touch of a button on his armor to anchor himself better into the ground. There was the tornado. It looked to be taller than old skyscrapers big cities used to have that contained as many as 100s of floors. It was wider than four average homes put together.

"Now!" said Jess. Seth aimed the Hydra then pulled the trigger. Out of the barrel came multiple bright lasers colored red, green, purple, silver, gold, orange, blue, and yellow. It sounded like lightning shooting from the barrel. Seth held on tight. The lasers shot high up into the sky then dove straight down into the top of tornado. The lasers then traveled through it bursting through all sides of the tornado's form. Everything seemed to move in slow motion. What seemed like forever was actually less than a minute.

The tornado slowly lost motion. Things it had sucked up along the way began dropping from it. There were tree branches, birds, rocks, grass, glass, mud, bricks, papers from who knows where, and small metal objects possibly from fencing or cars. These things were hurling fast through the air hitting the TSV. One little robin came right at the camera just missing it. Then the sun came out. It started sprinkling rain. The cicadas began singing.

Seth yelled into his helmet, "We did it again guys! Another success! Call in the State Guard!

Woo Hoo!"

"Okay Seth. Will do. That rocked!" Said Jess.

Charlotte turned off the TV with a big smile on her face. More lives saved again. The team made it look so easy, but it was really a complicated event each time. The doctor walked into Charlotte's room, "How are you feeling?"

"I'm doing okay. My ankle is sore. I still have a headache, but besides that, just fine."

"We just want to observe you this one last night. Is the physical therapy going okay with your ankle?"

"It's painful, but I'm still willing to do it on my own at home when I'm released."

"Good. Most people don't continue their therapy then end up with problems later including more surgery. The surgeon did a good job. He's always in surgery or he would have checked on you himself. You can follow up with me in a couple of weeks at my office." The doctor reached out lightly patting Charlotte on the shoulder with her slim small hand.

Charlotte smiled, "Thank you Dr. Webber."

"Try to get a good night's sleep. I know it's hard in here sometimes." The doctor walked out the door to visit her next patient.

Morning came quickly. A nurse came to Charlotte to give her instructions for home. Charlotte got out her phone. She looked at the nurse, "Can you send the discharge instructions to my phone? That way if I forget anything, I can look it up?"

The nurse tapped a couple of buttons on her laptop. "Yes, here you go. I am going to go over it with you verbally plus give you the hard copy of your stay on paper too."

"Great. Thanks."

It was around lunch time. Charlotte was brushing her hair waiting for her ride home.

"Knock, knock," her dad peeked his head into the room.

"Hi Dad. I'm glad to be getting out of here."

"I bet you are."

Charlotte limped over to the small closet. "Just let me put on my shoes then we can go."

"Your mother decided to wait in the car."

The nurse walked into the room with a wheelchair. "I'm your ride to the main entrance."

"Thanks." said Charlotte.

The three made it to the car. The nurse waved goodbye to Charlotte as Charlotte got situated in the back seat.

Charlotte's mom was in the driver's seat. She smiled at Charlotte, "Hi Charlotte. So good to see you up and around."

"Thanks Mom."

Charlotte's dad spoke up, "I don't know about you two, but I'm getting hungry. You want to stop somewhere for lunch?"

"Sure." said Charlotte.

"Me too." said Charlotte's mom. "Where should we go?"

"I'm in the mood for pizza." said Charlotte.

"Pizza it is." Charlotte's mom headed for a local pizza place.

It didn't take long to reach the restaurant. There were about 15 customers waiting at the bar to order.

"You two go ahead and get a booth. I'll order and be there in a minute." said Charlotte's dad.

They found a booth in a corner. There were flat screen TVs hanging from different areas of the ceiling, so no matter where a customer was sitting a TV could be seen. The restaurant smelled of garlic and tomato sauce.

Charlotte's dad walked up to the booth with a big pitcher of soda and glasses, "Here ya go ladies. The pizza should be ready in about fifteen minutes."

"Thanks Jim." said Charlotte's mom.

"No problem, Sarah," said Jim.

Jim and Sarah had been together for thirty-five years. Charlotte was their only child. Jim had met Sarah in high school. Jim hit it off with Sarah immediately. Jim had Biology class with Sarah. He sat behind her. He would whisper things to her to try to get her to go out with him.

"Hey Sarah, remember when I used to try to get you to go out with me in Biology?" Jim smiled at Sarah.

"Of course I do. How many times did it take before I finally said yes?" Sarah asked.

"Felt like at least a hundred," Jim laughed out loud.

"Could have been Jim. You were kind of cocky," Sarah laughed.

"How many times are you two going to go over this?" Charlotte smiled.

"Your mother says I was cocky. I wasn't cocky. I was just a nervous kid trying to get this gorgeous girl to say yes," Jim was looking right into Sarah's eyes.

"You were cocky Jim. You just didn't know it I guess." said Sarah.

"I remember when you finally said yes. I think it was day number twelve of trying and trying."

"You were definitely not a quitter," Sarah smiled really big.

Jim took Sarah's hand, "Do you remember what I said to you?"

"How could I forget?" asked Sarah.

"You going to tell me?" asked Jim.

"Go ahead Mom, tell him again," Charlotte was shaking her head while smiling.

"Okay, you told me that I was the most beautiful girl you had ever laid eyes on. You wanted me to give you at least one night out to prove you're a gentleman." said Sarah.

"Well, did you ever regret telling me yes? Was I gentleman?" asked Jim.

"Yes you were. And still are Jim." said Sarah.

Charlotte looked at how in love her parents were. She wanted that so badly. She wanted that with Seth. Seth was her dream man. The only problem was that every other woman in the nation was after him too.

The Tornado Wranglers Weather Jacked

One of the staff brought the pizza to their table, "Be careful. It's right out of the oven." There was steam coming off the pizza as the employee sliced it into pieces at the table.

Charlotte and her parents waited a few minutes to let the pizza cool. Charlotte noticed a couple of men walking up to the restaurant's door. The one in front looked like Jess from The Tornado Wranglers. He held the door open. Seth was behind him.

Charlotte was nervous. "Oh my gosh! Don't look now, but I think that's Jess and Seth from *The Tornado Wranglers*."

"Where?" Sarah turned around to look towards the front door.

"They just walked in." said Charlotte. "Do I look okay?"

"You look fine." said Charlotte's dad.

The next thing Charlotte knew, Jess and Seth were walking towards her booth. She could feel her face getting red. Her red face was blending in with her long red hair.

Jess looked at Charlotte, "Fancy seeing you here. We heard you got caught in a storm. You weren't chasing a story were you?"

Charlotte couldn't believe they were talking to her. She looked up with a smile, "No, actually I was just out driving. The report came on the radio while I was out. I had no idea I was going to be running from a tornado."

"We're glad you survived." said Jess.

Seth looked at Charlotte, "Your news channel said that you had been hospitalized."

Charlotte nodded, "I was in there for a few days. My ankle was the biggest thing. Some kind of metal got shot into it. The surgeon did a good job."

"We're glad it wasn't anything more serious." Seth said. "We like how tastefully you do your stories especially when it comes to us," Seth laughed.

"Thank you Seth." Charlotte said. "These two lovely people are my parents. This is Sarah and this is my dad, Jim."

Jess and Seth nodded at Sarah and Jim.

"It was nice to finally meet you Charlotte. It was nice meeting your parents too. Would you like my number?" asked Seth.

"Is it on the Internet or in the book?" asked Charlotte.

"Not the number I want to give you. Have you got a pen?" Seth smiled.

"I actually do. Here ya go." Charlotte handed Seth a pen from her purse.

Seth grabbed a napkin. He wrote down the private number to *The Tornado Wranglers'* headquarters, "Here you go. Put this in your cell. Call me sometime. We'll go out for a drink or something. Sound good?"

"Sounds good to me." said Charlotte. Her cheeks were getting hotter.

"We better grab a seat. I hope I hear from you soon." Seth walked away with Jess. They went to the other side of the restaurant to eat. As they walked to their seats, people recognized them.

People were shouting at them as they walked. One guy yelled to them, "I'll cover your lunch guys!"

"I didn't know they knew you." said Sarah.

"I didn't either." said Charlotte. "Was my face bright red the whole time?"

"It was, but I don't think those guys cared." said Jim.

"When do you think you'll call Seth?" asked Sarah.

"I really don't know. I'm glad they didn't sit down with us. I wouldn't have known how to act. It's not every day that two heroes walk up to me out of nowhere to say hello."

"It seems they have a mutual respect for you." said Jim.

"I am flattered. I do try to approach all my news stories differently than the other reporters. It seems they recognize that," Charlotte took a sip of her soda.

Jim looked at his daughter, "We've always admired you for that too. You're not a barracuda like some reporters can be. They'll do anything for a story. Everyone has a right to privacy. You seem to understand that. And you never make things up. So many reporters just make things up. They don't do any of their own research. People are turned off by that. That's probably why so many people watch you. They know you don't just read something that's given to you."

Charlotte grabbed a slice of pizza, "Thanks, Dad. We better eat this before it gets cold."

Seth kept glancing across the restaurant. He had admired Charlotte from afar for way too long. He couldn't believe he had finally just run into her out somewhere just out of nowhere. He wondered if he had been too forward with her. He hoped that she realized it wasn't an interview he wanted to do. He just wanted to spend time with her. He knew of a couple of quiet places where they could grab a drink to talk or just look at one another. Sometimes he would record her newscast to watch her spot in the news whether he was interested in the story or not. More than once Jess had caught him doing this at their headquarters.

"Are you glad I led you up to her?" Jess asked Seth.

Seth smiled, "What do you think?"

"It's not like you to go to her news station or look her up, so I thought I'd break the ice for you," Jess laughed.

"It *was* pretty smooth of you Jess. Just like your baby bottom skin," Seth laughed out loud.

"The ladies like my smooth skin. What gives?" Jess shook his head.

Seth laughed, "Just playing' with ya! You think she'll call me?"

Jess shrugged his shoulders, "Why wouldn't she?"

"I don't know. I guess I'll have to wait and see," Seth glanced across the restaurant at Charlotte.

Work & Dreams

Charlotte's parents dropped her off at home. Tomorrow would be her first day back to work since her encounter with the tornado. She was excited to get back to work. She did mostly the human interest stories. This included any tornado stories. She had no idea that Seth knew anything about her. The kind of news coverage *The Tornado Wranglers* got was usually worldwide news as well as local. Charlotte figured Seth didn't watch the local news, but was glad she was wrong about that.

She sunk down into her big Jacuzzi tub. The water was hot and soothing. Her ankle had some dull pain in it. She was hoping she would be able to walk normally by the time she met with Seth. She wondered what type of man he is. Does he like to dance? Does he like sports? Is he a womanizer or a gentleman? She put her bet on gentleman.

Charlotte got out of her tub. She wrapped herself in one of her dark blue bath sheets. It was so soft and warm. She loved how her towel warmer kept everything toasty. Her feet were comfortable too on her soft bath mat filled with gel that conformed perfectly to her small feet. She dried off and put on her long robe. It was warm too. She had left it hanging on her towel warmer.

She set her alarm for 4 a.m. She climbed into bed. She closed her eyes. Of course she immediately saw Seth when she closed her eyes. There was a giant tornado right behind Seth. The tornado must have been four stories high. It must have been half of a mile wide. Charlotte was standing close to Seth. His dark eyes were piercing down into her soul. His pupils became bigger the longer he stared at her. Time seemed to stop, but the tornado was still roaring above them.

"Take cover!" Seth yelled to her. Charlotte ran to a nearby ditch. Seth turned around to face the tornado. He secured his feet into the ground. The metal spikes in his boots dug deep into the earth.

Seth heard Jess's voice in his helmet. "We've had complete shut down here. You'll need to do this manually buddy. You can do it. Hold on tight. Hit override. Squeeze the trigger."

Seth held onto the Hydra. It jolted him a bit as all the bright colors escaped from the barrel. His leather gloves kept him from dropping the gun. Just as the lasers dove down into the top of the tornado, a small bicycle flew past Seth's head just missing him by inches. The tornado was dissipating as many things began falling to the ground.

"Get out of there!" yelled Jess.

"Gotcha!" Seth headed for the ditch where Charlotte lay. Just as he turned to run, the ground shook as a giant old oak tree hit the ground where he had just been standing. Seth was lying next to Charlotte in the ditch. He looked at Charlotte. She was unconscious. He took off his helmet as everything was quiet now.

Seth touched Charlotte's face, "Charlotte. Charlotte. Wake up. Are you in there?" Then he yelled her name, "Charlotte!"

Charlotte sat up in bed breathing really hard, "That was too real," she whispered into the darkness. She looked at her alarm. As usual, she woke up one minute before her alarm was about to go off. She quickly got dressed then went to the kitchen to cook a cheese omelet. The orange juice she gulped down tasted really good.

It was still dark outside. There wasn't any traffic this early in the morning. She enjoyed the ride into work on her motorcycle. Her work clothes were at work for any camera time. They had lockers for everyone. Changing in the restroom after her morning coffee was her usual routine.

She pulled up to the station which was a dome red brick building. Frank pulled up in his pickup truck next to Charlotte. Frank was her cameraman. They had worked together for about five years. "Are you going to get a new car?"

"Eventually I'll get a new one. Good thing I still have my motorcycle. I'd like to shop around for a while. I may get a truck instead."

"A big truck?"

"You never know. Maybe."

They walked into the news station. Frank walked off to gather his camera equipment. Charlotte went to the coffee pot. She could never remember which pot was decaf.

Laura looked at Charlotte's puzzled face. "The pot with the green spout is the decaf." "Thanks, Laura. I'm not sure why I can never remember that. I have to have caffeine. I'll avoid the green spout. I'm thinking green for go, so I get confused."

"No problem," said Laura.

"Do you think we'll get any bad weather today?" asked Charlotte.

"I just studied the radar. It looks like it'll be a calm day so far. We all know how quickly that can change though."

"We sure do. I had another dream about Seth last night." said Charlotte.

"Did he save you from your demise?" asked Laura.

"He sure did," Charlotte smiled.

"I wonder how many women dream about him coming to their rescue?" asked Laura.

"My guess is at least thousands," giggled Charlotte.

"You're probably right. I wonder if he lets that all go to his head?" asked Laura.

"I don't know, but I'm going to find out." said Charlotte.

"What do you mean? Do you have an interview set up with him or something?"

"Or something."

"What? Are you joking around Charlotte? It's not like you to joke about something like that."

"No, I'm not joking at all. I was out with my parents eating. He and Jess walked up to me then Seth gave me some kind of private number. He asked me to call him."

"Oh wow! How lucky is that? Where were you?"

"We were at The Pizza Place. Jess recognized me then led Seth over to our table."

Laura grabbed Charlotte's hands, "What did they say?"

"They admire my reporting."

"How did you get Seth's number?"

"He asked me if I wanted it. I asked him if it was on the Internet. He said that the number he was giving me wasn't on the Internet or listed in the book."

"Did you about burst or what?" Laura's blue eyes were glistening.

"I could feel my cheeks heating up." Charlotte giggled.

"You are so lucky. Have you called him yet?"

"Oh no. I don't want to seem anxious."

"But aren't you?"

"Yes, but he doesn't need to know that."

"When do you think you'll call him?"

"Maybe in a day or two."

"I need to get back to the radar. We'll be on air soon." Laura walked quickly toward the radar equipment. Her lean, long figure bounced lightly on the tile floor in the studio. Her blond hair was pulled atop her head with little curls coming off from around her ears.

"I need to get some more coffee then figure out what story I'm working on today." Charlotte said aloud to herself.

Charlotte sat down while drinking her coffee. She was looking at possible news stories to tackle. Her stories were usually live during the day then replayed for the evening news. She thought about interviewing recent tornado survivors. People loved those stories. She always started with footage of the tornado then ended it with people who had either hidden from the tornado or people who had lost their home or came close to losing their home. Normally people were at home at first sunlight. It had been a few days since the last tornado. Charlotte was thinking that by now the roads should be totally clear, so people can start checking out the damage.

Charlotte found Frank. "Hey, are you about ready to head out?"

Frank nodded, "Sure, what are we doing today?"

The Tornado Wranglers Weather Jacked

Charlotte took one last sip of her coffee, "Since it's been long enough to clear the roads, I thought we would go to some tornado damaged areas to see if we can interview any survivors."

"Sounds good to me. People always tune in to those stories." said Frank.

Charlotte realized she hadn't changed clothes yet, "Give me a few minutes to change."

"You mean you're not going in your motorcycle boots and leather gear?" smiled Frank.

Charlotte laughed, "I'll meet you out at the van in a minute, wise guy."

"Okay, I'll be ready," Frank nodded.

Charlotte got into her locker. There was a beige top with embroidery at the neckline that had lightly colored butterflies intermingled in the embroidery. She had tan boot cut jeans that didn't look like jeans. They were comfortable and looked more like dress pants. She went into the roomy restroom. It was designed for one person, but she didn't feel like she had to hurry because the station had five of these roomy restrooms for their staff. It took a lot of people to put on the news.

Once she was dressed, she looked in the mirror. She brushed out her long hair which fell to the middle of her back. Her hair seemed thin when wet, but was thick when it was dry. Her hair was a dark red, but not store bought. It was her natural color. The ends of her hair looked freshly cut. Her bangs went just above her thick eyebrows. She hated to pluck her eyebrows, so she didn't. Every once in a while she would get some stray eyebrow hair above or below her brows, so she would just shave it off. Her thick brows set off her big brown eyes. Her long eyelashes couldn't be seen very well unless she used mascara. She used a clear mascara to thicken them. Colored mascara was a pain because it would smear above and below her eyes. Her skin was a creamy peaches and cream. She always tried to stay out of the sun. She had a few freckles, but they weren't really noticeable. The camera loved her petite frame. She stood five foot eight inches tall.

Charlotte limped out to the van where Frank was waiting with the engine running, "I'm thinking we should hit the Fairington neighborhood. I heard it was one of the worst hit."

"Sounds good to me." said Frank.

Frank was a good looking cameraman. He had bright blue eyes. His hair was dirty blonde. In the summer, it lightened up from the sun. He was a thin man, but not muscular. He stood about five foot eleven. He had a deep voice that sounded like he should be on the radio. He was always open to whatever Charlotte wanted to do. He always did a good job filming her. He wanted her to look good because it made him feel good. Frank was a good driver too. He wasn't a lead foot, but could still get them to places quickly and safely. He always knew the best route.

The Tornado Wranglers Weather Jacked

"Oh look. That house had one wall ripped from it. I'm not sure how it is standing. Let's get closer to see if anyone is there." said Charlotte.

"Here we go." said Frank.

Charlotte hopped out of the van then began walking around as best she could with her sore ankle. She always looked for holes in the ground, live electric wires, and things hanging above from trees, and any animals or people that may have gotten missed when crews came to clean. She got closer to the house limping to the side where the wall was used to stand. "I'm not sure how this is possible. Okay, I see now. Someone has put supports in so the whole house doesn't fall to one side."

"Be careful Charlotte." Frank said.

Charlotte yelled into the house, "Is anyone home? Hello?"

"I thought I heard something." said Frank.

"Where?" asked Charlotte.

"Towards the back of the house." yelled Frank.

Charlotte slowly walked into the house where the wall was gone, "Hello?" She heard a clanking sound. She walked towards the sound talking a little louder, "Hello in there, this is Charlotte Coles from the news."

A lady was standing in the torn up kitchen, "Oh, hello. Yes, I recognize you." The lady's eyes went to the floor. Unidentifiable things were smashed into the tile floor. "I really need to sweep this up." She walked over to a cabinet to get a broom. She started sweeping up the mess.

"Were you here in the house when the tornado came?" asked Charlotte.

"I was."

"Do you mind sharing your story?"

"I'm still a little overwhelmed, but I don't mind. If it can help another survivor, I'd be glad to."

"Let me get Frank. He's my cameraman. Would it be okay if you lead us through the house to explain what happened?"

"I can do that."

Charlotte got Frank. Frank started filming, "Okay ladies, I'm rolling. We'll go live first then edit anything we add later."

Charlotte walked back into the kitchen where the lady was still sweeping up the mess. She looked into the camera, "This is Charlotte Coles, Channel 4 news. I'm here live with a survivor of the latest tornado outbreak. Can you tell us your name?"

"My name is Stella. Stella Hendrix."

"Stella, were you home when the tornado came through?"

"Yes. It was terribly loud. I felt lucky to have a basement. We have a finished basement, so I just walked down the stairs. I hid under our bar as soon as I heard the sirens."

"Who else lives here Stella?"

The Tornado Wranglers Weather Jacked

"My husband, but he wasn't home at the time. I was hoping wherever he was that he was safe. He happened to be on the way to the airport for a business trip."

"So you got under the bar then what happened?"

"I heard the loudest most powerful noise I had ever heard. It was like standing right under a roller coaster like one of those old fashioned kind of coasters they used to make from wood. It was scary. I heard all kinds of bumping and thumping. When it was over, it was almost like I had cotton in my ears. I could hear, but everything was muffled."

"Were you able to get upstairs once it was over?"

"It was a slow process. Something was against the basement door. The State Guard was walking around outside yelling for people. I started yelling for help as loud as I could. I decided to start kicking the door while I yelled."

"How long did it take them to get to you?"

"It felt like forever. I was so scared. A man was yelling to me that he could hear me. They were clearing the door."

"Do you remember his name? I don't remember his whole name, but his first name was Stephen. He with a crew of five people were trying to get to me. It took probably thirty minutes or so. My heavy duty metal patio sets blocked the door. The tornado turned them into tangled messes."

"What happened once they got you out?"

"I was so overwhelmed with joy, I cried like a baby."
Stella's face was suddenly streaming with tears. Frank did a close-up. Stella's eyes were a deep green. She wasn't wearing make-up. She had gray shoulder length hair and dark skin as if she had been to the beach. Her face was round.

"Are you okay Stella?" asked Charlotte.

"Yeah, I'll be fine."

"Do you want to take a break before we continue the interview?"

"Yes. Yes, that would be good. Thanks." Stella went into one of her bathrooms to blow her nose and pull herself together.

Charlotte looked into the camera, "We will provide more footage later tonight. Back to you at the studio."

Charlotte walked over to the open side of the house. Frank got a good shot of it while Charlotte stood in the opening.

Stella walked over to speak with Charlotte to finish the interview, "Luckily we know some contractors that will be here shortly to seal this back up. They already have it braced so the house doesn't fall on this side."

"That's great, said Charlotte. Your insurance company must be quick."

"Yes. I called them right away. They were here in no time." said Stella.

"Do you have tornado insurance?" asked Charlotte.

"Yes. We have the best. I'm glad we went with them." said Stella.

"It's okay if you want to tell everyone who you go with."

"The name is Total Storm Recovery."

"It looks like you'll probably be back in bed tonight."

"I hope so. I have some family coming over to help clean up the rest of this mess."

"Thank you for sharing your story with us Stella."

"Thank you."

"Okay. That's a wrap." said Frank.

Stella went back inside to finish cleaning up more rooms. Charlotte and Frank went into the van.

Frank was looking at the footage, "I think we have a good three minutes here. You think it will help anyone watching?"

Charlotte looked at Frank, "I think it will."

They headed back to the station to turn in their story for the evening news. Charlotte had to figure out what they could do for the next day.

Heroes Have Limits

Seth was at home watching the evening news. There was Charlotte again on Channel 4. She still hadn't called him. He wondered if she had lost the number. He decided to call Jess to meet at a local bar. A couple of beers would help him relax before heading back to headquarters the next day. A cheeseburger sounded good too.

They met at Harley's. There were about 25 people hanging out. It was a small place. The jukebox was playing the song Jukebox Hero. It played old vinyl records. Everybody enjoyed putting in a dime to hear their favorite classics. The bar owner had the jukebox restored to run just like it did back in the 1960's. For a quarter, you could hear three songs. The music was rock and roll from the sixties, seventies, eighties, and the nineteen nineties.

Seth walked up to the bartender, "Give me a bottle of Thriller. Thanks."

Jess walked up to Seth, "Hey, what's up?"

"Not much," Seth shrugged his shoulders.

"We just going to drink a couple then head home?" asked Jess.

"That's the plan," Seth held up his bottle of Thriller and took a sip.

"Don't look now. Here comes Krista. She's probably going to try to take you home again." Jess said to Seth.

"She's not my type. I don't think she'll ever get the message." Seth mumbled.

"I'd help you out Brother, but she's not my type either. Good luck," Jess laughed under his breath as he stood to Seth's side.

The Tornado Wranglers Weather Jacked

"Hey Seth. Whatcha doin? Gonna come home with Krista tonight?" She put her face within inches of Seth's face. Her breath smelled of a strong whiskey and cigarettes. She had on a micro mini skirt. It led nothing to the imagination. She definitely couldn't bend over in it without showing the world what lurked beneath.

"Don't think so Krista," Seth looked at her with no smile.

"Oh come on Seth. I'll be gentle. Let me feel those arms," Krista put her hands on each of Seth's biceps. As she lifted up her hands, her sleeveless shirt revealed an unkempt crop of black stubble on her underarms with a stench of body odor to go along with it.

Seth held his breath until her hands went down, "Krista, I think you've had too much to drink. Let me call you a cab," Seth reached for a landline phone on the bar.

"I've just had enough to loosen my tongue a little, that's all." Krista laughed into Seth's face. The cigarette smell made his stomach turn. Her bony face and dark yellow teeth were just too disgusting for Seth.

Seth was beginning to lose his temper. "Krista, I'm not interested!"

"Okay Seth. Okay. I get it. I'm not you're type. Whatever!" Krista marched outside while shoving a cigarette into her mouth trying to light it with a lighter. One of her long fake fingernails broke off falling to the ground. The pink polish on it was yellowed from the cigarettes she smoked.

"Great!" Krista yelled. "Now I need to redo my nails. Hope you're happy Seth!" she hollered behind her. Krista stumbled out into the parking lot. She stopped behind Seth's truck to smoke her cigarette. She was leaning against the tailgate and noticed it had big bold easy to read lettering on it. The bold lettering was Romans 10:9-10. As she puffed on her cigarette, she was trying to remember how those verses went. She knew it was pretty important, but she couldn't quite remember what it said. "When I get home, I'm checking that out," she said aloud to herself. About that time, a cabbie drove up to see if she needed a ride. Krista flopped herself into the back of the car to head home.

"Well Seth. Do you think she finally got the message?" Jess asked.

"I hope so. I'm tired of her touching me and breathing in my face. It's nasty. I've only ever seen her here when she's drunk. Who knows what she's like sober or if she's ever sober? That girl needs saved for sure."

"Sounds like you think she's never sober," Jess laughed.

Seth grimaced, "Seems that way, knowing that she lets herself get that way all of the time is a huge turn off for me."

Jess shook out a shiver that went through his body as he made an ugly face with his mouth while contorting his eyebrows,

"She'll find someone else to bother. Maybe someone more like she is. I just hope she never bothers me."

Seth grinned, "I think she's into hairy guys Jess."

"Let's hope so," Jess laughed aloud.

Seth and Jess finished their beers. They each got a cheeseburger with a soda to take home. No fries. They both started walking outside looking around to make sure Krista was gone. Jess got into his truck, "I don't see Krista anywhere. The cab must have picked her up."

Seth walked by Jess's truck. He looked at Jess, "I hope so. They say there's somebody for everybody."

Seth walked to his truck and got inside. He looked around at the sky. There were thousands of stars burning bright. He was thinking how it would be nice to share this moment with someone. He would love to park somewhere to sit and just stare at the stars. They wouldn't have to say anything to each other. They could just be happy sitting quietly with their thoughts, holding hands. It seemed the kind of women that chased Seth were not what he was looking for. Seth wondered what type of things Charlotte liked to do. He put the keys in the ignition and drove home.

Bad Timing

The tornado sirens were blaring. It was the middle of the night. *The Tornado Wranglers* were already driving around trying to find a tornado. They always tried to head off the tornadoes before they hit populated areas. The winds were exceeding 60 mph. The thunder was loud. It was booming every few seconds. The rain seemed to be going in every direction.

Sherry spotted a rain wrapped tornado on Doppler radar. Sherry had been working with *The Tornado Wranglers* for a couple of years. She radioed to Seth, "There's a rain wrapped tornado heading this way. Put on your glasses."

"Copy that Sherry." Seth put on his glasses by saying the word glasses inside his helmet. The glasses lowered inside his helmet covering his eyes, "I've spotted it. I'm ready when you guys are." Seth was having a difficult time keeping his footing. The ground had become too muddy even for the spikes from his boots. Hail started beating down in buckets the size of peas. The noise on his helmet from the hail was like hundreds of snare drums being struck over and over. Seth looked up. This tornado was long and skinny. It seemed to never end.

Jess was programming the Hydra from inside the TSV as Seth was positioning himself, "Seth, go for it. Everything is ready."

The Tornado Wranglers Weather Jacked

Seth squeezed the trigger. The bright lasers moved like flowing water from the gun's beam splitter inside its barrel. Just as the lasers reached the top of the tornado, Seth slipped in the mud. Both feet went out from under him. He was on his back before he had any time to react. Somehow he managed to keep the Hydra in his arms. While on his back, he readjusted his aim.

Jess was talking to Seth through the headphones in his helmet, "Good job Seth! Hang in there. Aim just slightly higher and that should take care of it!"

"Here goes nothing," said Seth as he aimed the Hydra slightly higher. His breathing was labored from all of the excitement.

The lasers from the gun disappeared bending then diving down into the top of the tornado. The tornado began to lose its rotation as lasers burst out of its sides. Debris began falling everywhere. Seth quickly rolled himself into the fetal position as quickly as he could to brace for any impact from the falling objects. Seth's team was watching from their TSV. Seth was much more vulnerable than they were. Those vehicles were like tanks. Seth let out a loud, "OOPH!" His body looked limp. He was no longer curled into the fetal position.

"You okay buddy?" asked Jess. There was no answer.

"Guys, he's not moving." whimpered Sherry.

Jess ran out to Seth slipping and falling twice suffering tremendous pain in his right knee. The hail had stopped. The lightning had stopped. There was a fine mist of rain coming down. Lying close to Seth's head was a metal scooter. It was the kind of scooter little kids ride that has one handle on it and kids power it with one foot. Part of the metal was twisted. There was a giant dent in Seth's helmet.

"I need a medic NOW." yelled Jess through the microphone in his helmet.

The medic was already on his way. He was trying hard not to slip and fall in the mud. Sherry called for an ambulance. The medic got to Seth. He pushed Seth's glasses back up into the helmet. Seth's eyes were closed. The medic's name was Scott. He would ride with *The Tornado Wranglers* whenever he could as a volunteer. "Seth, can you hear me? It's Scott. I'm going to take a look at you. An ambulance is on its way."

Seth started groaning.

"Hang on Seth. Help is on its way. Try to keep still. We don't know if you have any neck trauma. We'll get your neck stabilized once they get here." Scott said in a determined voice. Scott was holding Seth as still as he could.

It seemed like the ambulance was there in no time. "We don't know if he hurt his neck. There's a big dent in the side of his helmet. We need to stabilize his neck before we try taking off his helmet," Scott said to one of the ambulance medics.

The medics got Seth's neck stabilized. Scott pulled Seth's helmet off as gently as he could. There was no blood. There was nothing visible on Seth's head to show he had taken a blow. "This helmet probably saved his life. Let's get him to the hospital." Scott tucked the helmet under his arm as the medics put Seth on the stretcher.

Charlotte couldn't sleep because of the storm. She never heard any tornado sirens, so was happy about that. It wouldn't be very long before her alarm would be going off, so she decided to go ahead and get up. She had the day off work, but got up at the same time every day because she didn't want to break away from routine. Being late for work was unacceptable in her mind, so if she stuck with her routine even on her days off, she would be less likely to be late on days she did work. She went into her kitchen and started making breakfast. She turned on the little TV on her kitchen counter as she cooked.

"Breaking news. One of *The Tornado Wranglers* has been taken to the hospital. We don't have many details at this time. We know that he suffered a head injury and possibly a neck injury. We will provide more details as they come in."

"What?" Charlotte said aloud. How could this be she thought. She never heard any sirens. This must have been in a different part of town. She surmised it had to be Seth because he is the only one outside of the TSV. I can't believe this, she thought. I haven't even called Seth yet. I was so looking forward to spending time with him. Now he may be in the hospital fighting for his life? How is this even fair? Maybe it's not him.

Maybe it's one of the other guys. Maybe it happened when they were getting ready to leave to wrangle the tornado. I don't know, but I have to find out. All of these thoughts were going through her head fast.

"Breaking news update. We've just heard from Sherry Monroe of *The Tornado Wranglers*. She told us that Seth was injured fighting a tornado earlier this morning. Again, breaking news update: Seth of *The Tornado Wranglers* has been injured fighting a tornado earlier this morning. He has been taken to the hospital for his injuries."

Charlotte couldn't believe what she was hearing. Seth had never been taken to the hospital before not that she knew of anyway. She had no idea if they would let her in to see him or not. She decided to wait for more updates to see how bad his injuries were. Usually when there was breaking news about anything, the newscasters would just keep adding more and more information every few minutes. She may be able to find out more if she called her work. The reporter in Charlotte had a million questions that the breaking news just wasn't answering at all.

The station manager at Charlotte's work answered the phone, "Hello."

"Hey it's Charlotte. Who do you have on this story about Seth?"

"Oh hey Charlotte. We don't know much. Angela is on it. She is at the hospital talking with the other wranglers. As far as

Seth's condition, we don't have information on that yet. We do know that Jess was hurt too, but we don't know his condition either. I know you have the day off, but maybe you can find out more," suggested the station manager.

"I probably could find out more Dave, but I'm more curious for personal reasons not for a news story. If I go to the hospital, it's not going to be for work!" Charlotte exclaimed.

"We're all upset Charlotte. I understand. Don't feel obligated to pass anything onto Angela if you find out anything else."

"Okay. I'll be back at work tomorrow," Charlotte hung up the phone.

Charlotte put on her black leather motorcycle boots. The boots came up to her knees. She was wearing one of her black leather motorcycle outfits with it. She put on her helmet and took off towards the hospital. So many questions were going through her mind. She pulled into the parking lot of the hospital. There were about 100 people standing out in the parking lot. Some of them were holding signs facing all of the news cameras. One sign read, "Get Well Seth and Jess." Another sign read, "Seth & Jess Real Heroes." People were hugging each other. Some people were crying. There were news vans set up on the side street with reporters talking into cameras.

Charlotte walked down a ramp to get to the main entrance of the hospital. She went to the information desk. There were three people ahead of her. She heard a group of people talking and walking towards her. She looked up and realized it was the CEO of the hospital. The CEO was a petite woman in her fifties with short dark hair wearing a lanyard with hospital identification which included her picture. The CEO had a commanding but still feminine voice, "I need to get outside and make a statement. People need to move on so our patients can get in to the hospital." The people around the CEO were nodding their heads in agreement.

"Miss, can I help you?" asked a short round woman sitting behind the information desk. Charlotte realized she was talking to her. "Yes, I need to know which rooms Seth and Jess are in?" The lady behind the desk looked on the computer then looked up at Charlotte, "The hospital is only allowing family at this time due to the overwhelming response of people wanting to see them. We only have so much room for everyone. The CEO is giving a statement outside to the news crews if you want to listen in on that."

"I understand," said Charlotte. "Thank you for your help."

Charlotte walked back out into the parking area. She could see the CEO off in the distance near the news trucks. Rather than fight her way through the crowd to listen, she decided to go back to her motorcycle then head home to watch on television. In the back of her mind, she wondered why she thought she could just stroll in and see Seth and Jess. Maybe it was because she was a reporter who had access to other things in the past.

Charlotte wondered if Seth was able to talk and wondered if Seth would remember her. She couldn't believe he was hurt. There were many close calls over the years, but he had never been hospitalized.

Charlotte remembered a time a couple of years back when The Tornado Wranglers were having difficulty with a twin tornado. At first the tornadoes were right next to one another. Suddenly, one tornado decided to change direction as Seth was wrangling the one next to it. The footage of it was amazing. The lasers were high above one of the tornadoes and just as everyone started feeling comfortable, the other tornado had an energy burst where it pulled itself away from the other. The sound was quite deafening.

Due to Sherry's quick thinking in the TSV, Seth was able to regenerate the Hydra in a matter of two seconds. Seth immediately turned almost in rhythm with the escaping tornado. This is part of why a human needed to handle the gun. Gut feeling was needed not robots that sometimes malfunctioned. His eyes were firmly focused on both monsters. Time seemed to move in slow motion with no sound. All he could think of was getting the monsters down. Just half a mile from where he was standing was a huge farm of milking cows. He didn't want the farm destroyed.

Both tornadoes grew longer in a matter of milliseconds and the tops looked like giant dark wedges. Seth aimed then fired. The multiple lasers split into two separate shots hovering above the tornadoes that were now distanced about 50 yards apart from one another. There was some kick-back from the gun. Seth was knocked to his back then fell over to the side, but all the while he kept hold of the Hydra. The roars from the tornadoes turned into a whisper of a light wind. Objects were falling everywhere. Seth quickly scampered up as debris was falling.

Seth dove into a drainage pipe a couple of feet from where he was standing. As he dove into the gigantic pipe, a tree branch that was over five feet long with a circumference of at least eight inches whizzed by Seth's head putting scratches in his helmet that could be heard in the video footage. Everyone who watched the footage along with everyone who was actually there at the twin tornado site were certain that Seth had perished. Then over the headphones everyone heard Seth, "Whoa! What was that screechy sound?" Everyone at the twin tornado site cheered.

"Seth, Brother! We all thought you kicked it man!" Jess exclaimed over the microphone.

Seth hollered into the microphone, "Not me Brother! Don't know what that was, but I'm going to have ringing in my ears for days!"

"I need a nice cold one after seeing that. I think we all do!" Jess answered.

The Tornado Wranglers Weather Jacked

Jess unhooked himself from the seat in the TSV. He walked down to the gigantic pipe to help Seth out. The sun had come out. The dark clouds were almost a memory. Jess pointed over to the tree branch that just missed taking Seth's head off, "Brother, that's what had everyone all freaked out."

Seth walked over to the branch. It took both hands to pick it up. "Man, I bet this thing weighs close to a hundred pounds."

Jess walked over to Seth. Seth handed the branch over to Jess, "Feel the weight of this."

Jess grunted a little as he took the branch, "You aren't kidding, Seth. This IS heavy!" He threw the branch down.

Seth looked at Jess, "Jess."

"Yeah Seth." Jess replied.

"Brother, you got hair peeking out from your shirt sleeve! You need to get on that." Seth was laughing.

"Seriously Seth! Oh man!" Jess laughed while tucking the hair back up his shirt sleeve.

The State Guard showed up to see if anyone needed help. They were heading back from the dairy farm. A State Guardsman walked up to Seth and Jess, "There was only minimal damage at the farm. Your team did it again!"

Seth looked relieved. The winds from the tornadoes had only caused some broken windows and some equipment was scratched up from debris. Thankfully they had gotten there in time to save the farm.

That was probably one of the toughest wrangles yet because the tornadoes kept changing direction. Keeping up with it and figuring out what was going to happen next wasn't easy. The State Guard checked a few things and moved some debris off the road. The wranglers helped out cleaning up the mess.

Seth's luck didn't hold fighting this last tornado. He was unconscious in his hospital bed. Nurses and doctors were keeping a close eye on him. All they could do is wait to see if he would awaken.

Seth's grandmother was by his side. She was sitting as close to the bed as she could. She had her arms wrapped around his free arm. She had her head down on Seth's shoulder. She was thinking of the day she had to drag him away from his mother's casket at the cemetery. He was such a brave little boy through all of the funeral proceedings with many strangers he had never met who called out of respect.

When it came to leaving his mother in the ground, the braveness subsided to pure grief. Seth and his grandmother had stood in front of the casket for an hour and a half after everyone else had left. Seth stared at it intently as if hoping this was some grand joke hoping his mother would hop out of the casket to hold him then tell him it was all one big mistake.

The Tornado Wranglers Weather Jacked

His grandmother finally told him, "Let's go home Seth. You can come visit here as often as you like." She wrapped an arm around the boy and tried to walk with him. He was stiff as a board as he kept staring at the casket. For a little boy, he was very strong. "Come now Seth, we can't stay here all day."

"Why not grandma? Does it really matter? Who would know? I can't just leave her here. I just can't!" Then the tears came with the whimpers.

"Seth, let's go sit down on that bench. Let me tell you something." They slowly walked over to the bench. Seth just let his body go. He basically fell into the bench. His grandmother felt the metal bench give a little. His grandmother put her arm around him holding him next to her heart.

"Seth, you have been a very brave boy through all of this. It's a good thing that we found your mother. Some people never find their loved ones when a tornado strikes. We were lucky enough to find her to give her body a resting place that you can visit whenever you want. I loved her too Seth, still do. That never stops even after a loved one dies. Never. I am going to choose to remember all of the good times we had together. All of the times we went to the movies, all of the times we spent in the park watching you on the playground, the times we spent just talking about nothing in particular. You can do that too you know."

Seth sniffled a couple of times, "You mean like when she would tickle me or when we would go to the fair win prizes?"

"Yes. Focus on that. We're both going to miss her more than anything, but it doesn't mean we have to forget."

"I'll never forget my mom!" Seth sniffled some more wiping his nose with a handkerchief, "Never!"

Seth's grandmother nodded her head, "We'll get through this together. When I'm feeling sad, how about you tell me about a good time with your mom and I'll do the same for you." "Okay grandma. Grown-ups get sad too?"

"Why sure, there's nothing wrong with being sad. Now staying sad...that's another story."

Seth's grandmother realized she had been in really deep thought about her daughter's funeral. She looked up to see Seth still lying in the hospital bed. He was mumbling something in his sleep, but she couldn't quite make out what he was saying. She pushed the nurse button on the side of Seth's bed, "Seth, it's your grandma, can you hear me Seth?" Seth continued mumbling, but didn't seem to acknowledge his grandmother.

One of the nurses walked into Seth's room, "He's talking?"

"Yes he is," answered his grandmother. "That's good, right?"

"Yes, it is good. This is the first time we've heard him say anything. Let me put this in his chart."

The nurse was writing with a stylus on a small pad. "His doctor should be in a little later."

The Tornado Wranglers Weather Jacked

Seth's grandmother looked hopefully to the nurse, "I'll be here. I hope he wakes up soon."

The nurse replied, "Head injuries can be tricky. The helmet probably saved his life. All we can do is wait."

"I know. I'm trying really hard to be patient with him." said Seth's grandmother.

Seth could see the scooter coming right at him. The next thing he knew everything just went black. He was in total darkness. Then suddenly he had people all around him. He could hear them talking and feel them moving him around, but he couldn't respond.

Now he felt like he was stuck somewhere, but where? His body felt sore. He could smell, but couldn't quite figure out what the smell was. It wasn't familiar. Was he at home? No, it didn't smell like home. He felt something on his arm. He tried to open his eyes to look, but it was as if there were weights holding down his eyelids.

Now he knew what the smell was. It was like when you go to a laundromat when clothes have just come out of the dryer. He wondered why he would be at a laundromat. Then he thought about whether or not he was standing up or sitting down. He wasn't doing either. I wouldn't be lying down at a laundromat! Where am I? He began to panic. He began breathing hard. He tried harder to open his eyes, but for some reason he couldn't. The last thing he remembered was talking to Jess over his helmet microphone. He tried to yell Jess's name, but all that came out was a soft mumble, "Jess."

Seth's grandmother ran out into the hospital corridor. She found Jess. "Jess, I think he just asked for you!"

"I'm there," said Jess. He limped as quickly as he could to Seth's bedside. He was still recovering from his injury he suffered when he went to help Seth after the tornado. "I'm here buddy. Can you hear me Seth?"

Seth mumbled, "Where am I Jess?"

"You're at the hospital. You've been here since that last tornado."

"The scooter."

"Yeah, Seth. That kid's scooter knocked you out. Man, you don't know how good it is to hear you talk Brother!"

"Did we save some lives?" asked Seth.

"You know it!"

Seth's grandmother was standing in the background. "Seth, can you hear me?"

"Oh hey Gram." Seth's voice was getting stronger.

"I am so happy you're back Seth." his grandmother had a few tears welling up in her eyes as her voice broke up.

"Don't cry Gram. I'll be out of here soon. I promise." said Seth.

About that time, a nurse walked into the room, "Sounds like you're finally awake."

"Who are you?" asked Seth.

"I'm one of your nurses. My name is Lillian. Can you open your eyes Seth?"

"No, I can't. I have no idea why. It's like there's weights on my eyelids."

Lillian took a close look, "You've been out for a long time. It could be we just need to get the sleep out of your eyes. Let me see." She got down into Seth's face looking closely at his eyes. "Let me warm up a wash cloth for your eyes." Lillian went into the restroom then ran some warm water over a small white wash cloth. She wrung it out several times then walked over to Seth. "I think this wash cloth is ready to go. Are you ready?"

"Ready when you are." said Seth.

Lillian took a small portion of the cloth slowly wiping Seth's left eye. "It looks like you do have some junk in this eye. Let's take it slow."

Seth could feel the warm moistness of the cloth on his eye. It was quite soothing. Lillian had a gentle touch.

"Let that eye rest a little bit. Now I'm going to work on the other eye then you can try to open them both at the same time." She got a different section of the cloth and worked on his right eye. She carefully smoothed the cloth over his eye trying to get every little bit of sleep she could see.

"This looks good now. Slowly try to open your eyes now."

There was movement under Seth's eyelids. Then there was a small fluttering as he opened his eyes slowly. The lights were kind of bright, so he was squinting. "Could someone turn the lights down a little?" Seth asked.

"Of course," said his grandmother. She turned the slider down, so it wasn't as bright.

"Thanks." said Seth. "Now I don't feel blinded," as he opened his eyes wider. "So glad to see you guys."

"We're sure glad to see you too, buddy." said Jess. Jess bent down giving Seth a one-armed manly quick hug.

"Thanks Jess. How long have I been in here anyway?" asked Seth.

Lillian looked at his chart, "Looks like it's been a month."

"Whoa!" a whole month. "Did any storms come while I was here?"

"Actually, Seth, it's been pretty quiet. It's the strangest thing. Every time we thought a storm was going to form a tornado, it didn't." replied Jess.

"Seriously? You're not saying that to make me feel good are you?" asked Seth.

"No man! I'm very serious. I wouldn't kid about that. My knee is still healing. It was torn inside. That new tech surgery pretty much fixed it, but I'm still gimping around a bit. I was in line to take your place out front. I was worried I wouldn't be able to take it on, but there was no need. I practiced in the simulator, but never had to fight a tornado."

Dream Man Blues

Charlotte was getting home from work. She wondered if Seth would ever get out of the hospital. It seemed as if Seth had been in the hospital for an eternity. She dreamt of him more often since he was injured. She would wake up from each dream always wondering if she would ever get the chance to hear his voice again.

Charlotte walked into her living room, picked up the remote control to her television, switching it on to the news. She was hoping to hear that Seth had recovered, but there was nothing. She was trying to remember if Laura was home tonight or if she was at the fitness club. She decided to give Laura a call. Maybe they could hang out together tonight at Charlotte's house. Charlotte got Laura's voice mail, "Hey Laura. I was hoping we could hang out tonight. I've been thinking a lot about Seth. I need some advice. Give me a call if you get this early."

Laura wasn't at the fitness club. She was out shopping for new clothes. She liked to look her best when reporting the weather. She didn't feel her phone vibrate when Charlotte left her a message. She tried on one last outfit. She was happy with her finds. She grabbed her pants off the hook in the fitting room. Her phone was flashing. She decided to check her messages in the fitting room.

She listened to Charlotte's message, but wasn't sure if she wanted to call her back or not. Charlotte seemed head over heels for Seth, but just like everyone else had never spent any time with him. Laura didn't know if she would be able to handle listening to more of Charlotte's thoughts about Seth. They were all great thoughts, but until Seth was out of the hospital and Charlotte actually got to spend some real time with him to get to know who he is really is, they were just thoughts.

Laura didn't know if she could sit there listening to Charlotte go on and on about this dream man who may or may not ever wake up. Laura liked mixed drinks. She thought she could get Charlotte to have a mixed drink with her. The drink would help Laura relax while Charlotte went on and on. There was a quiet little bar not far from Charlotte's house. Laura decided to call Charlotte back.

"Hello Laura." Charlotte was smiling as she answered the phone.

"Hey Char. Got your message."

"Can you come over for a little bit?" asked Charlotte.

"I was thinking maybe we could go to that quiet little bar not far from your place." said Laura.

"You know I'm not much of a drinker Laura."

"Char, I know you don't drink beer, but they have some really good mixed drinks there. We could get one or two while we talk. If you feel like you get too much, you can always take a Buzz Kill. Now they have it in a chewable tablet if you don't want to drink one."

"I hope I don't need that. Um…Okay." Charlotte reluctantly agreed.

"I was thinking it would take me about thirty minutes to get there." answered Laura.

"Sounds good. I'll meet you in the parking lot outside the bar." Said Charlotte.

Laura grabbed all of the clothes then walked up to a register.

"Wow!" the cashier said. "You got a lot of nice outfits here. Treating yourself tonight?"

Laura stood looking into her wallet, "You have no idea."

The cashier smiled, "I got them all off of the hangers for you. Let me ring you up. That will be $242.36."

Laura handed the cashier the money using two $100 bills with three $20 bills. The cashier put the bills into a small machine that verified they were not counterfeit state bills. Most states in the nation had their own money that was backed by gold. It was hard to counterfeit the money, but businesses still checked it anyway. The cashier counted back her change.

Laura grabbed her two giant bags full of clothes lugging them to her car. She placed her bags in the trunk then took off towards the bar. Her radio was on music from the 1970's through the 1990's. She heard, "You can't hurry love. No, you just have to wait. Love don't come easy. It's a game of give and take." It was the 1980's version she loved. How ironic she thought. She was thinking about how Charlotte had been waiting forever on Seth to get better.

Charlotte saw Laura pull into the parking lot. Charlotte jumped down out of her truck then hurried to Laura's car door. Laura looked up with a smile. She opened the door. As she stood up, Charlotte gave Laura a hug.

Charlotte giggled a little, "You okay Laura?"

"Of course. Of course. How are you?" Laura leaned back taking in Charlotte's grin.

"Better now that you're here." Charlotte grabbed Laura by the hand to lead her toward the door to the bar.

They walked into the bar looking around for a good place to sit. "I'm a booth girl." said Charlotte.

"Me too." said Laura.

They found a booth in a quiet spot. There was music playing low in the background. There were maybe ten or twelve other people there.

The Tornado Wranglers Weather Jacked

They settled into their booth facing one another. Laura ordered them each a mixed drink. "Well," said Laura. "While we're waiting, what's on your mind?"

Charlotte smiled, "First, thanks for listening to me. You've been great listening to me go on and on about Seth since he got hurt."

Laura thought about how Charlotte just seemed so in love with Seth and felt guilty for not wanting to listen without a drink tonight. "No problem Char."

The waitress brought the drinks to the table. Charlotte was stirring hers with a straw, "This won't incapacitate me will it?"

"I'll keep a close eye on you Char. I'm not going to let them hang you. I'll give you Buzz Kill if I have to, so you can drive safely," Laura patted Charlotte's hand.

Dream Girl

Seth's grandmother was holding onto one of Seth's arms while he was speaking with Jess and the nurse. "Don't worry Gram," said Seth. "I'll be out of here soon."

"That's right." agreed Jess.

"The doctor should be in later today to speak with you," said the nurse. The nurse was looking at Seth's chart in the computerized notebook she was scrolling through. "Your tests look good, so I'm sure she'll have good news for you."

Seth's grandmother looked at Seth, "They did some MRI pictures while you were unconscious."

"Cool, maybe I'll get to see the pictures!" exclaimed Seth.

"You're definitely back Brother," smiled Jess.

"I'm ready to go work out." laughed Seth.

"Easy there," Seth's grandmother interjected. "Slow down. We need to find out what the doctor says before you go full throttle back into your life."

Seth looked disappointed, but agreed to slow down. "You're right Gram."

Gram looked at Seth, "You had a pretty frequent visitor here while you were out like a light. Jess told me you wouldn't mind."

"I wouldn't mind?" Seth looked over at Jess.

"Man, that reporter you like, Charlotte, kept stopping by to see how you were doing. I think she was here every day. I didn't think you'd mind. You're not mad are you man?" asked Jess with his eyebrows high and a goofy look on his face.

"Charlotte." said Seth. "I couldn't stop having dreams about her. Maybe that's why because she kept coming here?"

"Could be," said Jess. "I think that lady likes you because it had nothing to do with her job that's for sure."

"Really? So she didn't like go back to work to talk about me on camera?" asked Seth.

"Nope." said Jess.

"That's awesome!" Seth exclaimed as he rose a little bit off his pillow.

"Whoa! Take it easy there wrangler man!" Jess was laughing.

Gram was patting Seth's shoulder and smiling.

"Do you think she'll come see me today?" asked Seth.

"Most likely." said Jess. "It seems like she's here every day."

"Hey Gram, do you mind if I talk to Jess alone?"

"Of course not. I'll go get a snack."

Jess opened his eyes wider, "I knew you'd like that news."

"So Jess. Was she in here alone with me or what?"

"Yes she was. Like I said, I thought you'd be cool with it."

"You think she must be into me then?" Seth smiled.

"Why wouldn't she be Bro?" Jess shrugged his shoulders.

"Jess, she is the most beautiful woman I've seen. Even though I really don't know her, I get this kind of sting in me. You know what I mean?"

"I haven't been that lucky to feel that, but I think I get the idea."

There was a knock at the door. Seth looked at Jess, "You think that's her?" Seth kind of sat up a little.

It was the doctor. Seth and Jess laughed aloud.

The doctor looked at them, "Do I have something on my face?"

"No," said Jess. "We thought you might be someone else."

"Where's your grandmother Seth?"

"Oh, she went to get a snack."

"It's good to see you talking. Your tests are fine. Sometimes in head injuries, you simply need rest to recover. The helmet saved your life. You're going to be weak since you've been here for a while. Don't expect to just jump right back into wrangling. Okay?"

"What do you think I should do?"

About that time, there was a knock at the door.

"Come on in," said Seth hoping it was Charlotte.

In walked Gram, "Oh, hello, Doctor."

"I was just explaining to Seth that everything is fine, but he needs to take it easy at first. I was getting ready to tell him that I will release him from the hospital tomorrow. The helmet did save his life. It must be made of something pretty strong."

Gram looked at Seth. She bent down to kiss his cheek.

"I'd kiss ya too Bro, but a high five will have to do," laughed Jess.

"Okay Seth. You understand that you should hold off wrangling for a while, right?"

"I can hold off, but how long, what if they need me?"

"My knee is almost totally healed now. I'll hold things down for you until you can return," said Jess.

"Your knee?" Seth looked puzzled. "Oh yeah, you mentioned a surgery?"

"I came out after you in the storm. You didn't answer me. I had to see if you were okay. I slipped in the mud. The slip tore my knee. I'm almost totally healed now though. No worries."

"How long should Seth hold off?" Gram asked the doctor.

The doctor looked at Seth, "I'd like you to cut your workouts to a half hour then slowly build back up to your normal time. I know you guys work out whenever you can several times a day. One day the news said that you usually get in three hours a day. Your muscles need time to get used to it again. Once you slowly build back up to your normal time and nothing else comes up then I'll clear you to go back to work."

"I think I can handle that." said Seth.

"I want you to check in with my office once a week. You don't have to come see me unless something unusual is happening like dizziness, forgetfulness, or anything that doesn't seem right. Just call my office and leave a message with the nurse that you're doing fine. When you feel ready to begin work again, set up an appointment then I'll see for myself if you're ready. Deal?"

"Sounds like a plan." said Seth.

"Okay, let's shake on it." said the doctor.

Seth shook her small hand. Dr. Webber smiled, "I'll be going now. Don't let me see you on the news wrangling until you're ready." She pointed to Seth as she stepped out into the hallway, "We made a deal. Don't forget."

After the doctor left the room, the three looked at one another, so happy to know that Seth would finally be going home.

Jess spoke up, "Just so you know, we both got lots of cards, flowers, planters, and all kinds of stuff. There was no room for all of the stuff here, so you're going home to a whole lotta stuff. Your house is packed man! So is mine."

Seth seemed surprised, "Wow. Really?"

"I'm not joking. People freaked when we got hurt. They really are thankful for what we do." Jess was smiling.

Gram brushed Seth's hair away from one of his eyes, "I did the best I could to arrange everything neatly. I know how you like order. It is a little overwhelming when you first see it. The fresh cut flowers aren't around anymore, so I took pictures of that for you and left them on your camera."

"Thanks Gram."

"No problem. It gave me something to do when I wasn't here. I put all the plants in your little greenhouse. It's full now. There was this watering system I saw in a store, so it's not like you have to drag a watering can out there all of the time. It's on a timer."

"There's that many, you had to buy a system?" Seth asked.

"I figured once you saw it all, if you didn't want some of them, you could give them to others. I figured you would want to see it all. No big deal." said Gram.

"Thanks Gram. You are the best," Seth was smiling.

Jess headed towards the door, "On that note, I'm out of here. I need to go home for a while. I'm going to read some of my cards. The cards keep coming in. I bought a greenhouse for my plants too. People love us man. It's a great thing."

Daydream Believing

Charlotte was happy she only had a couple of drinks with Laura and was able to get home safely. If she drank much more than that, she would usually get a pretty bad headache. She didn't want to look or feel bad when she went to visit Seth the next day.

The next morning had Charlotte smiling about the dreams she had about Seth. She wondered how much the alcohol affected her dreams about him. In her dream, Seth was sitting up in his hospital bed talking with her like they had known one another for years. In her dream, Seth reached out with one arm, pulled Charlotte close to his face then slowly kissed her. One of her dimples on her lower back just above the back of her hips tickled deeply as Seth kissed her lips. Charlotte caught herself daydreaming about her dream. She laughed to herself as she brushed the dimple on her back with the back of her hand. She was hoping Seth really was a good kisser. In her dreams, he was amazing!

Charlotte usually cooked herself breakfast, but decided this morning, she would just grab a protein bar from her pantry. She filled up her water bottle at her fridge, gobbled down the protein bar, drank the water, filled up the bottle again to take it to the hospital with her.

When she couldn't think of things to say to Seth, she would read to him. She wasn't sure what types of things Seth was into, so she would load magazines onto her phone to read to him. Sometimes she would sit playing music over her phone too. There were other times Charlotte would just sit quietly looking at Seth intently trying to awaken him with sure willpower, but it never worked. She didn't see any harm in trying though. What would this man think of her if he had woken up while she was sitting there with her eyes intently focused on him? She had posed this question to herself on many occasions.

Charlotte wondered if Seth would even know who she was. Would Seth have amnesia? Would he be perfectly fine when he awoke? Would he be able to remember anything at all? Charlotte was hoping for the best. She had no idea that Seth was waiting to be released at the hospital that day. She was expecting to walk into his room with him sound asleep as usual.

Charlotte was almost to the hospital as her mind flashed back to that kiss from her dream. She had to shake it off then snap back to reality. I need to face reality, Charlotte thought, Seth may never come out of this. As she walked through the hospital, tears filled her eyes. She stopped at a nurse's station grabbing a tissue to dab them. The hallway was empty on the way to Seth's room. It was still pretty early in the day. Everyone must be with patients.

Charlotte walked up to Seth's hospital door. She knocked as she always had before entering, waited a few seconds then walked through. To her surprise, Seth's bed was empty. The lights were on. She heard water running from the bathroom. She wondered if she had walked into the correct room. She saw three plants under the plant light in the corner. She was in the right place. Should she knock on the bathroom door? Should she walk back out and come back in a few minutes? Her stomach felt like it was in her chest. Then she heard a woman's voice come from the bathroom. The bathroom door opened, a nurse was walking backwards out of the bathroom. Then Charlotte heard Seth's deep voice, "I feel much better now. Thanks for your help."

"No problem," said the nurse. The nurse turned her head to see Charlotte was standing in the room, "Looks like you have company, Seth."

Charlotte peeked around the nurse just as the nurse was turning Seth around in the wheelchair to face Charlotte, "Um, I can come back if this is a bad time."

"We were getting him a shower. He finally got to use that nice shower in there. I just rolled him in there and waited to make sure he didn't need anything. It's fine."

Seth was smiling really big at the sight of Charlotte, "Hi Charlotte."

The nurse began to walk away, "I'll let you two catch up. If you need anything, just let me know."

"Thanks again. I feel much better," Seth nodded to the nurse.

The nurse left the room.

At the exact same time Seth and Charlotte said, "It's good to see you."

Charlotte laughed, "You owe me a soda."

"I have no problem with that," said Seth. "The doctor said I can leave today."

Seth started tapping his hand on the arm of the wheelchair. It was a nervous habit he had when he didn't know what to say next.

"I'm so glad you remember me." Charlotte said.

"I couldn't forget a lady like you." Seth replied.

Miserable Nicholas

Nicholas Nading had been anxious for a storm to develop. There hadn't been a tornado since Seth and Jess got hurt. Nicholas loved to chase storms. He got as many up close videos and photos as possible. He did this even though The Tornado Wranglers had cameras on their vehicles. Nicholas was sort of a nuisance since he didn't take any safety precautions during the storms. It's almost as if he thought he was invincible during the storms or he had a death wish. Nicholas was never killed or hurt because Seth always was there to save him. He sold the footage he would get to television shows and weather magazines. People still enjoyed flipping through paper magazines. Some people read things online just out of convenience.

The only time Nicholas was maybe a little sober was during a storm. The rest of the time he was pretty much drunk or drinking to get drunk. His body didn't cooperate with him sometimes when he was sober because it was so used to the years of alcohol pumping through it.

Mr. Nading was a tall man who stood six foot three inches. He had bright red hair, red eyelashes, and red eyebrows. His body hair was bright red as well. He used to have a canine tooth on the right side of his mouth, but that tooth was knocked out when he passed out after a bender one night. When his face literally hit the floor, the canine tooth was knocked back into his mouth. He woke up wondering what was in his mouth spitting the tooth out onto the floor.

Nicholas wasn't married. He lived in a small one bedroom efficiency apartment. He had one thing in his life that he cared more about than himself and it was his cat. He took much better care of the cat than he did of himself. The cat's day consisted of many naps plus eating two gourmet cans of food a day. Nicholas would brush the cat daily. The cat would purr during the brushing sessions then eventually fall asleep. Nicholas called the cat Midnight for two reasons. The first reason was because he had found the cat at midnight outside of a bar. The second reason was because the cat was a dark black color with tiny dots of white all over its fur like stars in a midnight sky.

Nicholas was sitting at a bar eating some chips while watching the news. Laura was on the news talking about how some rain would be coming through the area, but there would be no storms.

Nicholas slammed down his drinking glass, "Where the hell are all the storms?" he barked aloud.

The bartender shot Nicholas a look of disapproval, "Settle down or get out!" he growled.

Nicholas put both hands up in the air, "Okay, okay. Sorry. So sorry." He calmed down, put the glass up to his lips, throwing back his head as he snarfed down the rest of the alcohol.

There were always drivers outside the bars. If there wasn't a driver, a person could call to get one usually a few minutes away. Drunk driving was basically nonexistent. Nicholas didn't want to be hanged. Sometimes Buzz Kill didn't work right away for him, so he always made sure he used a driving service if he knew he had too much to drink. The driving services used drivers that had never used any kind of alcohol or drug in their lives. It was big business. Many people who were sober their entire lives made an excellent living driving for these services. In most cases it was their only job because they were busy early afternoon into late at night.

Some of the bars had sleeping rooms for free if a person didn't have extra money for a driver or Buzz Kill. Most people only used the sleeping room by force when a bouncer decided they had too much. The sleeping rooms weren't made to be comfortable. It was usually just a tiny room with a few cots inside. Not many people ended up in them.

The driver dropped Nicholas off at his apartment. He staggered into his living room. He fell into his recliner which sprung way back leaving Nicholas flat on his back. That was a mistake. He felt a burning in his chest as vomit traveled into his throat. He jumped up over the arm of the recliner barely making it in time to the toilet. Some of the alcohol vomit spilled out through his nostrils. It burned and it stunk making him heave even more violently into the toilet. He wiped his mouth with the back of his hand while flushing the toilet. He groaned as he was holding his stomach. He decided to splash some water on his face while looking in the mirror. His light green eyes were bloodshot. The drinking had taken a toll on his looks making him appear ten years older than his biological age. He hadn't gotten too ugly, but he was on his way there with the constant consumption of alcohol.

There was a familiar feeling brushing the tops of his feet. It was Midnight. "Oh, hey Midnight. What are you doing?"

Midnight looked up at Nicholas then meowed.

"I know what you want." Nicholas walked over to a cabinet pulling out Midnight's cat brush. The cat meowed again as soon as she saw the brush.

"Okay, let's go over there, so I can brush you."

They walked over to the couch. Midnight jumped upon Nicholas's lap. The cat purred with every little stroke of the brush. She began kneading Nicholas's thigh.

"You're a happy girl now. I wish a storm would come. I need to make some more money. I'm running out of pictures to sell."

Midnight fell asleep on Nicholas's lap. Nicholas tilted back his head falling asleep while holding the cat.

Second Date

Charlotte couldn't believe that Seth was sitting in front of her. They had decided to grab a soda at a little hole in the wall on a side street in town. They were sitting in a booth staring at each other.

The Tornado Wranglers Weather Jacked

"Again, I'm so glad you remembered me," Charlotte said to Seth in a quiet tone. Her eyes were locked deep into Seth's eyes.

"Well, Charlotte you're quite unforgettable," Seth smiled.

Charlotte could feel her cheeks getting warm. She wondered if her face was turning red.

Seth touched her rosy cheek with the inside of his fingertips, "No need to be embarrassed." Charlotte felt a tickle from her face as it raced down her back into one of her dimples on her lower back. His touch did wonderful things to her. His hand was warm and soft.

Seth was wondering if it was too soon to kiss her. He could see that she was wearing some type of lip gloss that smelled like fruit. Probably cherry flavor, he was thinking.

Charlotte wondered if he would kiss her or was it too soon for a kiss. They had only been at the restaurant for maybe an hour.

"So, how was I when I was basically in a coma?" Seth asked.

"You didn't move or say anything, so I would just talk to you or read to you. Sometimes I would turn on the television. I kept trying to will you awake thinking that maybe if I thought it hard enough that my brainwaves would somehow affect yours getting you to wake up. I tried that many times to no avail," Charlotte let out a little giggle.

"I appreciate the effort," Seth took one of Charlotte's hands into both of his hands, "Do you mind?" He gently pulled her hand to his lips kissing the top of it.

The biggest rush went from Charlotte's hand clear down through her toes. It was almost like the first hill on a roller coaster. His touch drove her absolutely wild. The chemistry is definitely here, she was thinking in the back of her mind.

Their concentration with one another was broken by the sound of a bell on the door when a couple entered the restaurant. The couple looked to be in their early eighties and they were holding hands. Charlotte and Seth both studied the couple as they walked by to get a booth.

"Wow," said Seth. "Did you see them? I wonder how long they've been together."

"You never know." said Charlotte.

A little head peeked around the side of the booth. It was the woman from the couple who had just walked by. She looked at them, "sixty years."

Charlotte looked at the woman, "Wow!"

"You're telling me," said the older woman. "He's the only man who would put up with my crap." Then the woman laughed aloud pulling her head back into her own booth.

With that said, Seth and Charlotte had huge smiles on their faces. They both leaned forward across the table. Their lips met for a few short seconds. They both got that crazy tickle in their stomachs. They both pulled away at the same time then just sat back holding hands across the table.

Seth licked his lips. Definitely cherry lip gloss, he thought to himself.

"I hope I didn't wear the sour kind," Charlotte giggled.

"What?" Seth asked. "Oh no," he laughed, "It's just regular cherry."

"Sometimes I can't tell the difference," Charlotte grinned.

"How long would you like to stay here? Do you want some food?" asked Seth.

"Sure, what are you going to get?" asked Charlotte.

"I usually just get a cheeseburger with a soda."

"Okay, I'll take a cheeseburger too then." Said Charlotte.

"You want another soda too?" asked Seth.

"Of course." Charlotte put her hand over the top of one of Seth's hands. The charge she felt throughout her body was undeniable. She had never watched Seth eat. She hoped he wasn't a lip smacker. She hoped he turned out to be the kind of guy who closes his mouth when he eats not smacking his lips all over the place. She was holding in a giggle at that thought. His teeth looked so nice. Surely he brushed them often. They looked straight, white, and clean. She wondered if any of them were fake. They didn't look like veneers. He seemed so genuine. He always smiled when he spoke which seemed genuine too.

The cheeseburgers came. They were third pound burgers, so they were huge! Charlotte hoped she could eat it all. Seth almost seemed to read her mind, "You know, if you can't eat it all, you can always save it for later," he said softly.

That eased Charlotte's mind. "Yeah, I was just wondering if I could finish it all in one sitting," she laughed as she picked up the burger with both hands. Her small hands barely fit around the thing.

Seth bit into his burger. He chewed quietly glancing at Charlotte while she ate. Every once in a while, he would ask her something like what she does for fun and that kind of thing. Nothing big. But isn't that what makes life? Little things count so much, Seth thought.

Charlotte finished her soda, "Do you know if they have free refills here?"

"Oh, yes they do," Seth said after swallowing the last of his burger. Seth lifted up his hand looking over at the waitress.

The waitress hurried over, "Is there something you two need?"

"Could you refill our sodas, please?" Seth asked.

The waitress smiled at Seth, "Of course, no problem." The waitress got a pitcher of soda pouring them each another glass.

They both reached for their glasses finishing off every drop with their straws.

The Tornado Wranglers Weather Jacked

Seth looked at Charlotte smiling as usual, "Do you have any plans for the rest of your day?"

Charlotte just wanted to spend the rest of the day with Seth. "No, how about you?"

Seth made a suggestion, "I was hoping you would say that. Maybe we could drive out to a quiet spot to sit for a while. Or we could take a walk or both?"

"Sounds like a plan," Charlotte stood up to leave with her leftover burger wrapped in a small bag.

"Hold on a second. Seth was thumbing through his wallet. I'll take care of this bill, but I want to make sure I give the waitress a good tip."

Charlotte was thinking about how she always made sure of that too. She knew how hard waitresses worked for their money. When Seth was done, Charlotte grabbed his hand without even thinking about it to walk out the door.

The older couple was still in the diner eating their lunch. The man looked at his wife, "They are going to be together for a long time."

His wife nodded, "I know."

Seth and Charlotte drove to an area that overlooked nothing but the tops of trees. They quietly sat together in the truck admiring the landscape. This is great, Seth thought. She hasn't said a word. I don't feel like I need to talk constantly.

This is awesome, Charlotte thought. He hasn't said a word. I don't feel like I need to talk the whole time. Charlotte was snuggled up to Seth's side as they held hands. Charlotte was thinking about how safe she felt with Seth.

Seth was thinking about how nice it felt to have someone to just sit with him. He liked having someone who can just be.

The Gang's All Here

So far, no one among the public was aware of Seth being released from the hospital. Scott was at The Tornado Wranglers' headquarters. He was checking the supplies that he may need if someone gets injured. Everything seemed in order. Scott had been a paramedic for years. He loved to help people. He always remained very aware of everything around him no matter what he was doing. When Scott found out the Tornado Wranglers needed volunteers, he was the first one in line to apply. Any volunteer had to go through a stringent screening process. Volunteers were given a personality test, a test in a simulator that simulated bad weather conditions, and each wrangler spoke with the volunteers just to see whether or not they were a good fit with the team. Scott was around 5'11", dark hair, dark eyes, short dark beard, and had a medium body frame. Scott passed everything with flying colors. Not everyone did. Some people wanted to volunteer just for the notoriety of it. Those type of people were turned away.

The Tornado Wranglers Weather Jacked

Gram drove over to Tornado Wranglers' headquarters to let Scott know that the hospital had released Seth. Scott, Gram, Jess, and Sherry decided to decorate the inside of the headquarters to welcome Seth back. There were Welcome Back signs everywhere including Seth's favorite place, the workout room. There were colorful balloons floating around. Gram gave people whistling noisemakers along with rattling noisemakers. Gram called Seth on his cell phone. Seth heard his cell phone buzzing. He pulled the cell out of the console to see who it was.

Gram's picture popped up on his phone. "Sorry Charlotte, I need to take this."

"No problem." Charlotte answered.

"Hey Gram, what's up?"

"Seth, I was wondering if you'd like to stop by headquarters. Your fellow wranglers wanted you to see some changes they made while you were gone." Gram was smiling at the others standing around her at headquarters as she spoke. She gave a wink to Jess.

"Sure Gram, I guess. Will it take long? I'm hanging out with Charlotte right now."

"You can bring her along." Gram suggested.

"Well, I'm not sure she would be much interested." Seth looked at Charlotte, "Would you mind stopping by my headquarters? There's something they want to show me."

Charlotte shook her head, "I don't mind at all."

"I'm sure it won't take long," Seth took some soft strands of Charlotte's hair that had fallen onto her face. He gently tucked them behind her small ear.

That gave Charlotte tingles from her head down to her feet, "Fine by me," she replied.

"Can you give us about thirty minutes to get there Gram?" asked Seth.

"That works." Gram replied. She hung up with Seth to let everyone know they would be there in about thirty minutes. There were about twenty people there to welcome him back. Each person was someone who was close to Seth or had worked with Seth in wrangling.

Charlotte and Seth pulled up to headquarters. Everyone had parked far away then walked over, so it would be a surprise. Scott was outside waiting for them. He wanted to look like he was working on something when they pulled up. "There's Scott," said Seth. "Let's go up to see what he's doing." Charlotte started releasing her seat belt. As Seth was getting out of the truck, he looked at Charlotte, "Wait right there a second." Seth hurried around the front of the truck to open Charlotte's door for her. He took one of her hands to help her down out of the truck.

As Charlotte stepped down from the truck, she looked up at Seth, "Thank you Seth." "Anytime Charlotte." Seth let her hand go as they walked up to Scott.

Scott gave Seth a quick manly hug, "Good to see you up and around."

Seth was grinning, "Scott, this is Charlotte."

Charlotte put out her hand to shake Scott's hand, "Nice to meet you Scott."

"Nice to meet you, Charlotte. Haven't I seen you somewhere?" Scott asked Charlotte.

"Probably on television," she replied. "I'm a reporter."

"That's right, are you doing a story on Seth?" asked Scott.

"Not at the moment. We're just hanging out." Answered Charlotte. Seth put an arm around Charlotte.

Scott smiled, "Oh, I see. Let's go inside you two."

The three walked into the headquarters. There was a loud, "Surprise!" people were blowing their noisemakers, rattling noisemakers, and throwing golden confetti everywhere.

Seth looked around at all the happy faces, "Well, hello everyone!" Seth said with a laugh as he brushed a couple of pieces of confetti from his hair.

Gram walked up to Seth then kissed his cheek, "All of us are so glad to see you finally out of the hospital."

"I'm happy too Gram," Seth hugged Gram. Everyone had formed a circle around Seth and Charlotte.

Sherry kissed Seth on the cheek, "It's been too long. We're all so happy to see you back." Sherry had tears welling up in her eyes.

Seth pulled Sherry close to him. He whispered in her ear, "I'm going to be fine. Don't worry." With that, Sherry pulled back wiping the tears from her striking green eyes.

"You better be fine, Seth. Things can finally get back to normal around here. So are you going to introduce your hospital friend?" Sherry asked.

Charlotte put out her hand to shake Sherry's hand, "I believe we would pass one another in the hospital halls from time to time. I'm Charlotte. I guess I didn't realize you were there visiting Seth. Hello."

"Have I seen you on the news?" asked Sherry as they shook hands.

"Probably. I do the local news. It's nice to meet you." Charlotte felt kind of awkward unaware of what type of relationship Sherry had with Seth.

"It's good to meet you too. I guess it just didn't feel right introducing myself in the hospital. I never could stay very long, but I did see you in there a few times. I'm Sherry Monroe."

"You're a wrangler too aren't you?" asked Charlotte. "I think I've heard your voice on worldwide news when you're talking to Seth over the helmets."

"That would be me." Sherry smiled. "I'm very protective of the guys."

"That's a good thing." Said Charlotte.

The Tornado Wranglers Weather Jacked

Seth gave Sherry a look as if to tell her to back off, "Ladies, let's go find some punch. I'm sure there's some around here somewhere."

There was a loud siren sound coming from outside. At first everyone stiffened up thinking a tornado was in the area.

"It's okay everyone, just the monthly test." Jess announced.

"I kind of panicked for a second," said Seth. "I'm not sure when I'll be able to go out again."

"It's cool," said Jess. "I think if necessary, I could do it. I've been practicing."

More than Friends

Laura Lovell was sitting in her apartment browsing the Internet. She was thinking about the talk she and Charlotte had the other night at the bar about Seth. Laura kept trying to find information on one-sided love. She thought if she tried hard enough, there would be a way for her to help Charlotte if Seth never woke up. Laura read ten or eleven stories about women who wouldn't give up on coma patients, but the coma patient never woke up. Some women still stayed at the hospital. Others gave up and went on with their lives finding another man. Laura was pretty sure that Charlotte would never give up on Seth. She knew Charlotte had gone to see Seth earlier that day. She imagined that Charlotte was still there reading to Seth or putting on the television for him or maybe Charlotte had some music playing. Laura prayed as she often did for Charlotte and Seth to finally be together. "Please Heavenly Father, let them be as one. Amen," Laura whispered softly.

The party was over at The Tornado Wranglers headquarters. Charlotte and Seth had wandered into the area where the men sleep during their shifts. Seth had his arm wrapped around Charlotte's waist. He steered her over to a sofa near the TV. "We can sit here for a minute if you want." Said Seth.

"Okay," said Charlotte. They sat down together. A few people could be heard left in the building talking about the impromptu surprise party. Charlotte's mind was still processing all of the people she met. It was a small party, but most of the people she had just met. Sherry stood out in her mind. "Sherry seems like a nice person," Charlotte said quietly.

"She is," said Seth. "She is kind of like the mother hen around here. She's always watching out for us even when we're not fighting storms."

Charlotte smiled. "I wasn't sure if she was someone you were seeing or what when she first met me."

Seth laughed out loud, "Sherry? Oh, we're just friends. Always have been. It must've been the look she gave you, I guess."

Charlotte nodded. Seth turned his head to bury his face in Charlotte's soft red hair. He took a long, deep breath, "Your hair smells so good! It's really soft too."

Charlotte was enjoying his face in her hair. Her head was tingling. She was smiling while leaning her head more into his face.

"Oh, that's real nice," Seth whispered.

"Well you two, I'm heading out," Gram was standing in the doorway.

Charlotte and Seth both jumped up as if young teenagers caught doing something wrong.

Seth walked to the doorway, "Thanks so much for the party Gram," then hugged Gram tightly.

"No problem. It was spur of the moment. I'm glad some people showed. You two don't stay up too late. You need your rest," Gram turned away to head out.

Charlotte ran up as Gram was heading out, "Nice spending time with you. I enjoyed the party. I'm glad I got to meet some of Seth's friends."

Gram looked back as she headed outside, "I know, they were glad to meet you too. Goodnight."

Seth grabbed up Charlotte hugging her, "I'm glad you got to meet them too." They stood there silently hugging.

Scott walked up to the two, "Oops, didn't mean to interrupt. I'm heading home too."

Seth kept hold of Charlotte while looking over at Scott, "No problem. See you later Scott. Have a good night."

Scott walked out the doors.

"I don't hear anyone. Is anyone left?" Charlotte asked quietly.

They began walking around to see if anyone was there. "Somebody must be here." said Seth. "There's usually at least two of us that spends the night. We're not here all of the time, but most of the time. We take turns spending time at home." They walked into the kitchen area where Jess and Sherry were sitting at the table talking. "We were starting to think nobody was staying the night." Seth said.

"We're going to," said Jess.

Charlotte looked at Jess, "I guess I didn't realize you sleep here."

Jess explained, "It's more for security reasons. People get curious. They come around wanting to look at the TSVs and meet us. That's why we take turns going home. I'm going to go get ready for bed. See you later."

"Yeah, it's been a long day," said Sherry. "I think I'm going to hit the sack too." She walked up to Seth and hugged him. She looked over to Charlotte, "Goodnight."

"Goodnight." Said Charlotte.

Seth looked at Charlotte, "I better get you home. Good thing we dropped your truck off earlier."

"Yeah, I'm ready to hit the hay too." Charlotte replied.

The Consequence

Nicholas Nading woke up with a loud throbbing in his head. The night before he had way too many shots of whiskey. The driving services were all booked up. He didn't feel like waiting until a driver was available again. The bar he drank at that night didn't provide sleeping rooms, but the bar did have plenty of Buzz Kill on hand. He ended up chewing up two handfuls of Buzz Kill in order to drive home. It was the most Buzz Kill the bartender had seen anyone chew up at one time.

It had been a while since he had seen any hangings on TV. When the laws went into effect several years before, there was one hanging after another televised. There were only three states that did not have the hanging laws. They were dangerous states to live in, so not many people lived in them. Only undesirables lived in those states. They were viewed as freaks by the world for choosing their "do whatever you want, when you want, and how you want" type of existence.

Nicholas lived for drinking, but he wasn't willing to take the chance driving drunk then hanging for it. The very first time he saw a televised hanging, he saw it at home. He wasn't aware it was going to be on TV. He had just come home from photographing some tornadoes. He was sitting on one end of his couch and was getting ready to head into the kitchen to heat up a TV dinner. There was an alert on the TV. It caught his attention, so he sat back down then turned up the volume. He thought it was a weather alert. He was hoping to go out to shoot more storm pictures. Instead, a news anchor came on stating the first female was about to be hanged for drunk driving. The news anchor explained the woman was 32 who had a record of driving drunk before the new laws were in place. The news anchor went on to explain that they would televise her hanging. The anchor advised viewers to change the channel or turn off the TV if this was something you did not want to see.

Out of curiosity, he continued to watch. Nicholas had never seen anyone hang let alone a woman hang. There was a crowd of people around the platform where the woman would be hanged. There were no children in the crowd. A small van drove up next to the crowd. Two male officers got out of the van. They opened the back door to lead the woman to the noose. She was very thin. She had light black hair that was tied back in a ponytail. The long ponytail touched the top of her tailbone. She had dark blue eyes that were glistening from her tears. Her skin was very pale. Her unpolished fingernails were chewed down to the nubs. She was looking at the noose hanging that was slowly swaying in the light breeze which blew harder as she was being escorted up to the platform. Her reality began to set in. Her small five foot frame began wriggling. She was trying to get away from the officers. The policemen had a firm hold of each of her skinny arms. She began screaming, "I don't deserve this!"

A strange man from the crowd with dark gray eyes and sunburnt skin approached the young woman, "You must obey the law." He bent down over her small frame kissing her cheek then walked back into the crowd. The woman had no idea who the man was. His kiss made her skin crawl.

The woman tried to walk up the thirteen steps to the platform. Her legs kept giving out. The police had to keep lifting her up to her feet. She sobbed quietly looking down at the ground. They placed her under the noose.

Several people in the crowd had signs they were holding up. None of the signs supported the woman. Some signs read, "Think Before You Drink" and some read, "Drive Sober."

The crowd was silent as a tall lanky man with long black hair walked onto the platform. He placed the noose over the young woman's head. He took hold of her ponytail pulling it through the noose so her hair would not interfere with the hanging. He looked at the woman, "Have you anything to say before your punishment?"

The tears would not stop streaming from her eyes. Her tears were splatting onto the pine wood platform below her feet. The woman looked into a news camera screaming, "I could drive just fine!" Then she began crying softly while looking down.

The man spoke, "Ally Smithe, you have been convicted of driving while impaired. Your blood alcohol content was point three eight per the blood draw at the scene of the crime. Another blood draw at the jail confirmed this finding. This is far beyond the legal limit to drive. Although you believe you would not have hurt anyone, we must follow the state law punishable by hanging." Ally kept shaking her head.

The lanky man continued, "If you would like, you may have a bag over your head or you can choose to die without one. Do you want me to cover your head?" He was holding a black velvet bag in one hand. The crowd was still silent as they watched.

Ally answered the man choking on her tears, "NO."

"Okay then. In three seconds, we are going to pull the floor so you will fall. You may or may not die immediately." Ally was still shaking her head. "Three, two, one." The floor fell out from underneath her. Her neck made a slight cracking sound most likely unheard by the onlookers. She struggled kicking her petite legs for what seemed like two or three minutes then she was gone. She wasn't able to grab at her neck because her hands had been cuffed behind her back. The crowd looked on in disbelief in complete silence, bowing their heads as Ally's lifeless body hung. Nicholas couldn't believe it either. He turned the TV off. He thought about the fact that if they'll

hang a young woman, they'll hang anybody. He got a bottle of whiskey out of the cupboard. He threw back three shots and went to sit back down on his couch. He knew he could never drink and drive again.

Comas & Best Friends

Laura Lovell was at home completely unaware that Seth was out of the hospital. She was in her walk-in closet looking at her newest finds from the local dress shop. She was trying to decide what to wear to work in the morning. Laura liked to wear a different outfit each day. All of her clothing was sorted by color. It really didn't matter which color she wore. She made everything look good. The only color she didn't have was green because she would become invisible to viewers on TV due to using the green screen when giving her forecasts. She had many skirts and shirts that she could mix and match. She even had dresses that were reversible. She finally decided to wear a nice blue dress that brought out her piercing blue eyes. Getting everything ready the night before work made things so much simpler. She usually had to be at the news station pretty early in the morning when most people are still in bed.

Laura could usually get by on about five hours of sleep. She had a treadmill in her bedroom. Each night she would walk on it for an hour before going to take her bath. This was no leisurely walk she took either. The treadmill had different programs so she could walk up and downhill. Sometimes she would run to get up the hills a little more quickly. She liked to stay lean. Laura began thinking about Charlotte again. She talked herself into a decision that she would definitely talk to Charlotte about Seth's coma and how he may never come out of it.

Seth took Charlotte home. He again helped her step out of the truck. He walked her to her door. Charlotte could feel her phone buzzing in her small purse that was hanging on her shoulder. She looked at Seth telling him whoever it was could wait. Seth hugged Charlotte then whispered in her ear, "Let's do this again real soon." Charlotte looked at Seth. She gave him a soft kiss. Seth's eyelashes brushed her face as they pulled away from one another. Without a word, she smiled at Seth, unlocked her door, and Seth walked away backwards as she walked inside. She slowly closed the door as Seth turned to walk away. Charlotte locked her door, kicked off her shoes, and walked into her bedroom. She had almost forgotten someone had tried to call her. She couldn't stop thinking about Seth. She thought about his soft touch. She wondered how his long eyelashes would feel on her lips. She was hoping to get a chance to do that soon!

Charlotte reached into her purse looking at her phone. It was Laura who called. Since it might be about work, she decided to call her back. It rang a couple of times then Laura answered, "Hey Char!"

"Hey Laura. Sorry I didn't get your call earlier. I was in the middle of something."

"Oh, no problem. I was just thinking that we should have dinner together tomorrow. I know you'll probably want to go to the hospital first to see Seth, but maybe after that?"

"Actually Laura, I have some great news!"

"What is it?"

"When I went to see Seth, he wasn't in bed. He was actually in the shower. I couldn't believe it! They released him today. Only a few people know I guess. Isn't that awesome!" Charlotte was giggling with delight.

"Oh…" said Laura feeling relieved. "I had no idea. Yes. Of course, that is. That's awesome news Char!"

"I just spent most of the day with him. We really hit it off. He wants to see me again. The chemistry is definitely there Laura. Definitely." Charlotte was giggling again. She was beyond happy.

"We don't have to have dinner tomorrow if you already have plans." Laura was feeling excited for Charlotte.

"Oh, no, Laura. We didn't make any plans yet. We just talked about hanging out again sometime soon. We can have dinner. No problem at all. I always enjoy it when we're out together. You're my best friend." Charlotte replied.

"Think about where you might want to eat. We'll talk more about you and Seth tomorrow after work." Laura said.

"You know I'm up for anything. Someplace quiet would be nice so we can talk. I have so much to tell you! I'll let you get some sleep now Laura."

"Okay, goodnight Char."

The two hung up. Now Laura's mind was spinning again. She was elated for Charlotte. "Thank you God," Laura whispered as she fell to sleep.

The Cat's Meow

Nicholas Nading was out driving around hoping a tornado would form soon. The fact that no tornado had touched down in weeks was highly unusual. Every time it seemed one would happen, it just turned out to be a thunderstorm with no rotation. People were more interested in tornado footage than footage from thunderstorms. Nicholas would stop from time to time to see if any drones were in the sky. Drones sometimes meant that a tornado was about to form. The information from the drones was sent back to meteorologists for more accurate lead time to warn everyone. There weren't any drones in the sky today. It seemed like today was going to be a bust.

Nicholas had some money saved up, but was uncomfortable with using up his savings for everyday living. He decided to go hit a bar anyway. He could use a driving service or take some Buzz Kill if he drank too much. There were only about ten people in the place. There were televisions everywhere. There was a small area where music was playing. He decided to go to where the music was playing. A waitress with tiny little jean shorts and a tiny red t-shirt that was too small for her walked up to Nicholas. "What'll you have today?" she asked. She blinked her dark brown eyes a few times. Her false eyelashes were definitely too long. She was petite and skinny except for her chest.

Nicholas looked up from his chair. The woman's chest was just a few inches from his face. It was almost impossible for him to look at anything else, but he did try to look at her face without much luck, so he glanced down at the drink menu. Without looking up he ordered a whiskey on the rocks.

"Coming right up." The waitress walked back to the bar to have the drink made.

Nicholas was listening to the music while swaying his head to a country song. The waitress came back with his drink.

"That was quick. Thank you Hun! I'll leave you a nice tip." Nicholas smiled at her as she sat the drink on the small round table. All of the sudden there was a loud swoosh! Then there was continuous banging. It sounded like millions of tiny balls were hitting the roof of the bar.

Nicholas jumped up knocking over his drink. He fished some money out of his jean pocket then ran over to the waitress handing it to her, "Don't worry about the spilled drink. I gotta go!" By the time Nicholas got out the door, the hail had stopped, but it was raining giant raindrops. All that could be heard was rain. He jumped in his jeep turning on the radio. His wipers could barely keep up with cleaning the windshield. Nicholas was about twenty minutes from home. He turned up the volume so he could hear over the pouring rain.

The State Weather Service has issued a tornado watch. If you live in the Greenland neighborhood, keep an eye out. Conditions are favorable for a tornado. "That's my neighborhood," Nicholas said aloud. Nicholas needed to turn around to head in the direction of his neighborhood. He found a gravel road off the main road to turn around. He had no idea if he had remembered to put his cameras in the jeep. There was a small storage space in his jeep where he kept them out of sight. He would have to look for them once he got to his neighborhood. He couldn't drive very fast because it was almost impossible to see. It seemed an eternity. Finally the rain let up, but high gusts of winds kept pushing his jeep from side to side.

There wasn't anyone out on the streets. They must have all taken cover. It was dark and windy. The wind was blowing something across the street just as Nicholas was driving through. It was a huge branch that had been ripped from a tree. It hit the jeep almost flipping it, but luckily the jeep ended up lopsided with two tires on the branch and the other two tires on the road. His seatbelt stopped him just short of hitting his face on the windshield. Nicholas let out a sigh, "Whew!" His breath fogged up the windshield where his face almost hit. Nicholas could see his neighborhood. He could see where his apartment should be.

He could also see The Tornado Wranglers. Jess was out in the street. The tornado was nowhere to be seen. The wind decided to stop. The clouds in the sky broke up. The sun was trying to peek through from behind a solitary puffy cloud. Jess saw Nicholas walking towards him.

"Hey Nicholas! You just missed the tornado. We got here right at the last minute."

Nicholas looked past Jess, "Where's my apartment?" Nicholas started running. He was tripping over debris as he ran.

Jess tried to stop him. Nicholas kept running. All he could see was a pile of concrete and bricks where his apartment should be. Nicholas started yelling, "Midnight! Midnight! Midnight!"

Sherry ran over to Jess, "What's going on?"

Jess looked puzzled. "Nicholas is yelling for someone."

Nicholas was screaming at this point, "My cat. Where the hell is my cat?"

Jess began walking with Nicholas, "We'll help you find your cat."

Sherry didn't think they would find the cat. The tornado they fought was strong. It took extra energy to break it up to get rid of it. Jess had done his best, but the tornado was just too much.

Scott ran up to Nicholas, "What's the cat's name again?"

Nicholas was digging through bricks with his hands, "Her name is Midnight. She's all I have."

"Don't worry man, we won't leave here until we find her." Scott reassured him. Nicholas nodded his head and continued digging through the bricks.

The other wranglers were walking around looking up in trees and checking between buildings that had survived. Some residents began appearing as they felt it was safe to come out from their basements or shelters. All of Nicholas's neighbors were accounted for. Everyone began searching for Midnight.

A policeman was driving through the area. He stopped because he could see everyone was searching for something. "Do you need more help?" the policeman asked Scott.

Scott pulled his head out from an area where he thought the cat may have been hiding. "Yes, we're all looking for a cat named Midnight."

The policeman smiled. I may have someone who can help. He opened the back door of his car bringing out a German shepherd who was wearing a vest. The policeman walked the dog over to Scott on a red leash, "This is Lucy. Do you think the cat is buried in the rubble?"

Nicholas overheard them talking, "I think she could be anywhere."

The policeman shook Nicholas's hand, "I'm David. This is my K-9 Lucy. I think she'll be able to sniff her out."

The Tornado Wranglers Weather Jacked

"I actually have one of Midnight's toys in my jeep if you think that'll help?" asked Nicholas. "I keep it in there for the Sunday drives we take together."

The officer looked surprised by that. He had never heard of a cat taking Sunday drives. "Okay, let's go get it. We'll hold onto the toy while Lucy sniffs her out in case she loses the scent." They carefully walked back to the jeep through all the debris in the road. Nicholas pulled out this little red cloth mouse from the glove box that Midnight had played with hundreds of times. The toy jingled as he handed it to David.

David looked at Lucy, "Lucy, smell this girl. Take a big whiff." The dog sniffed it. David reached down to unhook her leash, "Go find her girl!" At first the dog looked around as if it wasn't sure which way to go then she held her head up high as if searching the air for Midnight's scent. The dog was slowly walking around stopping here and there then she picked up pace. She had been searching for twenty minutes. Nicholas was thinking the worst. People were still yelling for the cat. There was a small area where nobody had gone to yet. The dog was trying to dig at the bricks then started whining and barking. David walked up to Lucy, "Did you find her girl? Is she down there?" The dog barked several times then sat down.

David looked at Nicholas, "I think this is it."

Scott ran up, "Did she find Midnight?"

David nodded his head. Nicholas and Scott started picking up bricks throwing them to the side. There was a small hole at the bottom of the bricks. Nicholas looked at Scott, "I think that used to be my living room floor."

"Midnight!" Nicholas yelled down into the hole. "Midnight!" Nicholas reached down into the hole. He moved his hand around as much as he could in the cramped space. His fingertips felt something soft. "Midnight!" he yelled again. He couldn't quite get his hand where it needed to be. "I feel something soft, but only with my fingertips. I don't know if it's her."

Scott looked at Nicholas, "Let me get in there. I'll make the hole bigger without hurting her." Scott took his hand grabbing a piece of the wood that used to be the floor. He pulled up as hard as he could to make the hole bigger. He managed to rip it about three inches wider pulling the wood up and out, "There, now stick your hand down in there."

Nicholas put his hand down through the hole. This time he was able to feel Midnight's tummy.

"I feel her. I'm going to pull her out slowly." He wrapped his hand around the cat slowly lifting her out of the hole. By that time everyone had figured out they had found her. Everyone was watching as Nicholas pulled her out, "Midnight." Nicholas's eyes welled up with tears. "Midnight, can you hear me?" He pulled the cat closer to him with both hands. The cat seemed lifeless.

Nicholas looked at Scott, "I don't think she's breathing. I'm not sure."

Scott gently took the cat, "Let me see her." He put the cat on her side on a patch of soft grass. He put his head to her chest, "I think I can hear a heartbeat. Let me try something." Scott opened a black plastic case pulling out a tiny plastic mask. He put the mask over the cat's nose and mouth. "She may just need a little oxygen. She may not have had much air under there." Everyone was silent as they watched, "Just give her a minute."

Midnight's eyes were closed. She was outstretched on the grass with the tiny mask over her face. Nicholas was sitting in the grass next to her shaking his head.

Out of nowhere, "Meow!"

Nicholas couldn't believe it. Everyone cheered.

Nicholas began petting Midnight while Scott was still holding the mask on her face. The cat stayed put taking in the oxygen.

"We'll let this stay on a few more minutes just to make sure she's okay then we'll check her out," said Scott.

Nicholas nodded his head. He was stroking Midnight's head happy she was alive. A few minutes later the cat began to purr. She slowly got to her feet then walked onto Nicholas's leg kneading it. Nicholas laughed, "She's making biscuits!"

Scott laughed too, "Well, look at that. It wouldn't hurt to take her to the vet just to make sure all is okay."

Nicholas reached up to shake Scott's hand, "Thank you Scott."

Scott shook hands, "No problem. When I first saw you here, I thought you were here to cause trouble. I didn't know you lived here."

Lucy walked over to Midnight and licked her head a couple of times. Nicholas patted Lucy and thanked her for her help.

David squatted down to pet Midnight, "Nice cat you got there."

Nicholas looked up, "Thank you. Thanks for stopping to help."

David nodded his head, "I'm going to get Lucy back to the station now. Have a good night." It occurred to Nicholas that he had nowhere to stay. His apartment was gone.

One of his neighbors walked up to him, "We have room if you need a place to stay. We just live a block over. Our house wasn't hit. You can stay as long as you need to."

Nicholas wasn't used to people being nice to him. He didn't know how to respond. At first he was quiet.

"Okay. Lead the way." Nicholas accepted. He carried Midnight in his arms as he followed the woman.

They reached the woman's home. She turned around and looked at Nicholas, "My name is Jen and my husband is at work right now. His name is Larry."

The Tornado Wranglers Weather Jacked

"Are you sure your husband is okay with another man in his home?" asked Nicholas.

"Larry is a very giving person. He trusts my judgment in character too. I already called him before I offered you the room anyway. Somehow I was able to get through on my cell phone to him."

"As long as he's okay with it. Do you have kids or pets?" asked Nicholas.

"All we have is an aquarium. It's in our living room. You can stay here until you're able to find something else. Did you have insurance?" asked Jen.

"Yes, I did. I forgot about my jeep. I'll have to walk back so I can drive it over."

Nicholas walked back to his jeep forgetting two wheels were atop a big branch. When he got back to his jeep, there were people working on the branch with chainsaws. Once they got it sawed up, he'd be able to drive away.

The last of the branch was sawed up. A crane had come in to steady the jeep, so the jeep could softly land on the road. Crane businesses were big since there was always somebody somewhere that needed help. Most people would file a claim with their storm insurance to cover the expense of it. Most crane companies reasonably priced their services because there was always enough work for everyone. Nicholas gave the crane guy his storm insurance card, the guy swiped the insurance card on a gadget on his phone and let Nicholas know there was no copay for today. Nicholas was able to hop in his jeep to drive away.

Jess and Sherry were talking about how quickly the tornado popped up in Nicholas's neighborhood. They didn't have the time to wrangle it the way they wanted to. Some tornadoes were called Pop Ups. There was a watch for the area, but no rotation seen ahead of time, so the tornado formed as quickly as it moved through the neighborhood. The Tornado Wranglers had come across more and more of these over the years. Nobody was really sure what it meant. The good thing is that the tornado wouldn't last long enough to cause widespread damage. Usually when a Pop Up would happen, that would be the end of it and no other storms would follow. The wranglers studied footage of these Pop Ups time and time again to try and figure out why they wouldn't last very long. It was frustrating for them because sometimes they couldn't get there in time to prevent damage. Some people saw this as a sign that tornadoes may come to an end in the future.

Girl's Night Out

Charlotte was getting ready to meet Laura for dinner. Her thoughts were filled with Seth. She was hoping to tell Laura all about Seth. He was such a gentleman. Charlotte was thinking about how he seemed like he was recovering well. She was so happy he could now talk with her. The days of reading to him while he was in a coma were finally gone.

Laura was getting ready to meet Charlotte at the restaurant. She was going over in her head all of the things she wanted to say to Charlotte. She was going to start with how they have been friends for several years now. She felt close to her as if they were sisters. She wondered what Seth was like and if Charlotte's first impressions of him lived up to the type of man Charlotte had dreamt of.

Charlotte pulled up in the parking lot at the restaurant. The place didn't seat many people. It was small and quiet. They served Mexican style food that could be pretty spicy. Charlotte and Laura both liked spicy food. They usually added hot sauce to their orders even if it didn't really need it. Laura drove up next to Charlotte and got out of her car. Charlotte jumped down out of her truck to give Laura a big hug. They were both smiling. "Let's get inside for some appetizers," said Laura.

The two walked into the restaurant. The hostess walked them back to a quiet corner table and handed them menus, "Someone will be with you shortly."

"This is a nice quiet little space," Laura grinned.

"Yes, I think this will do. I have so much to tell you about Seth." Charlotte replied.

The two began looking at the menu while they crunched on some tortilla chips with salsa.

"Oh Char, this looks good. It's got peppers, onions, chicken, rice, and some beans wrapped in a flour shell. Let's get this."

"Sounds good to me." Giggled Charlotte.

"You're in an awfully good mood," Laura grinned at Charlotte.

Charlotte looked Laura straight into her eyes, "I have Seth on my mind. I'm wondering if he is the one I've been looking for."

"I see," Laura grinned.

"Laura, I think you're going to like Seth. You are my best friend. It would mean a great deal to me if you would come meet Seth when you have time."

Laura was taken aback, "I can do that. Tell me about this Seth guy you're so smitten for."

Weather Modification?

Jess was in his apartment shaving away all of his hair on his body. Seth was visiting him. Seth yelled from the living room, "You ever gonna get all that hair off of you Jess?" Seth was laughing loudly.

Jess walked into the living room wearing a muscle shirt and a pair of shorts, "The only hair the ladies like on me is on the top of my head." Jess was grinning ear to ear as he pointed to his head, "The ladies love this blonde hair. It's not going anywhere." Jess laughed.

Seth looked at Jess's head. He got up then wrestled Jess to the ground. He got Jess in a headlock giving him a noogie.

"Hey now, quit messing up the locks," Jess was laughing while he was trying to release himself from the headlock.

"Alright, I'll let you go this time," Seth was laughing as he released Jess.

"It won't be much longer. I won't have to shave again. That thing I use slowly gets rid of all the hair permanently," Jess was smiling as he rubbed his bare arm.

"Yeah, yeah," remarked Seth. "The ladies love your bare nakedness. Right."

"They do. Anytime I go on a date, it's one of the first things they do is remark on my baby smooth skin. It's awesome!" Jess laughed.

Seth sat down in front of the computer, "I came over today so we could go over some weather data."

"Okay, let's take a look," said Jess.

"We need to figure out what is affecting the tornadoes if anything." Said Seth.

"It's rumored they've been modifying the weather for years. Nobody can figure out who they are though. Maybe that's why we're seeing more pop up type tornadoes that are hard to catch." Said Jess.

Seth zoomed in on a section of the map where lots of tornadoes hit each year. "We need to figure out if any weather modification has gone on in this area lately. I'm thinking in the last six months. This may tell us if it's affecting tornado production." Seth typed in the words, number of weather modifications.

The computer spoke aloud, "Define weather modifications."

Seth sighed, "Evidently it is just a rumor. The computer doesn't even know what that means which seems unlikely. Sounds fishy to me. Let's try this." Seth then typed, show weather that is purposely changed.

The computer spoke aloud, "I have no results for weather purposely changed."

Seth then typed, show weather in this area that doesn't coincide with the season.

"Why don't you just speak to the computer?" asked Jess.

"I don't like speaking to those things. I'd rather type it out." Seth laughed. "Why do you have this thing set up to speak anyway? It's creepy. Only people should be speaking. Machines speaking is just not right," Seth shook his head.

"You better type something different cuz it has no idea what you're talking about," laughed Jess. The computer had no idea what Seth meant by weather not coinciding with the season. Seth hit enter again to ask again.

The Tornado Wranglers Weather Jacked

The computer was thinking then spoke again, "There have been two hundred and sixty three weather events not common to the area in question."

"What?" Seth looked at Jess. "That's a lot! That has to mean something."

"It means we're screwed is what it means. That's a tiny area with way too many weather events," Jess said shaking his head.

Seth typed in, "Show number of tornadoes in past three years."

The computer spoke, "There have been an average of twenty tornadoes each year in this area of uncommon weather."

Jess asked what type of uncommon weather happened in that area.

The computer answered, "The uncommon weather that most often occurs in this area is lightning, wind, and snow."

"Snow? There? That is weird." Jess said.

"It doesn't make sense." Said Seth. "Maybe weather modification is real, but why would someone jack with the weather? I've always wondered about that. I'll put in a request for some state wide information. We'll sit down for a few days during our down time to take a look at all of it. It may take some time to go through it all. Stopping tornadoes is a good thing, but preventing them altogether would be even better."

"I'm with you my brother. I agree," Jess nodded. "I hope it is just a rumor about weather modification. The fact the computer didn't know what it is tells me someone probably is jacking with it, but why?"

Seth shrugged his shoulders, "Remember back when the federal governments around the world were overthrown by the people? We were just teenagers. We didn't understand any of that at the time. Now we know all of the ugly things that were being done to the people worldwide. Those governments didn't run things for the people. They ran things for their greed and control over everything. Maybe someone is trying to pull something like that again. I really don't know for sure, but I know we'll figure it out. We may be the best wranglers in the country, but we can't do this forever."

"Yeah, I guess we can't stay young forever. It's either figure out how to stop these things from forming or we'll be training replacements when we get a little older." Jess laughed. "We may not have these ripped meat suits that we have now," Jess laughed a little harder.

Seth started laughing as well, "My meat suit is still gonna be ripped when I reach ninety my brother! I may not be as quick on my feet when I'm ninety, but I guarantee I'll still be ripped. Seth flexed his arms, "And… if these tornadoes are still whipping around, I'll be out there chasing them. I just won't be wrangling them anymore."

The Tornado Wranglers Weather Jacked

Jess was laughing so hard, he was doubled over. "I'm with ya my brother. I'll be right beside ya" Jess stopped laughing, "I have another thought on how these storms pop up. What if it's not really a storm? What if it's something else? But, by the time everyone gets to it and sees it, we think it's a tornado."

Seth was confused. "What do you mean? What could cause something to appear to be a tornado?"

"I don't know for sure. I think we would need to see if we can find some archived radar footage that has the drone videos combined with it. I'll have to find out how far back we can go. For years they destroyed the radar with video footage after six months for some reason. I can't remember when they started archiving it all." Said Jess.

"Interesting." Seth nodded his head. "Yeah, let's dig into that."

"What we'll need to do is apply filters to the footage. I'm not sure what we're looking for. I have a feeling that what we find is going to surprise us." Jess commented.

Seth thought for a minute, "Let's get right on that. Not every tornado has the drone video footage though, but most of them do. Sometimes the tornado destroys the drone before the footage can be received by the radar computer."

Jess asked the computer to pull up radar drone video footage from various dates of known Pop Up storms.

Seth thought of something, "Tell it to also pull up storms that did not pop up. Maybe if we compare the radar drone video footage of each, we may see something."

"Okay." Jess agreed. "Computer, run radar drone video footage of regular storms for comparison."

The computer showed the footage Jess asked for.

"Computer, magnify images 2 times." Jess stated.

Jess and Seth both looked closely at the images. They didn't see anything unusual in either storm.

"Computer, magnify images 3 times." Said Jess.

"You know, I'm not seeing anything on this either. Let's apply a filter now." Said Seth.

Jess nodded, "Computer, apply filter A to both images."

Both wranglers looked at each image. They still were not seeing anything unusual.

"I'm going to apply another filter with that filter." Said Jess. "Computer, overlay filter B onto filter A to both images."

Both men stared at the images for a moment.

"I'm not sure what this is here," Seth pointed to a round object in the image of the storm.

"Let's find out." Said Jess. "Computer, isolate this image." Jess circled the image with his stylus on the screen, "Computer, magnify isolated image."

"Oh, okay. That is a hub cap from a car. Probably got picked up by the tornado." Seth said.

"Yeah, that's definitely a hub cap. We see those all the time." Jess concurred.

Seth felt his cell vibrate in his pocket. "Hold on a second. I'm getting a call." Seth saw that it was Charlotte, "Let me take this Brother."

"Sure, I'll be in the laundry room." Jess said.

"Hey Charlotte." Seth was smiling as he answered her call.

"Seth, hey. Hope I wasn't disturbing anything." Charlotte said.

"No, not really. We were just doing some research on something. What's up?"

"I want you to meet my best friend. I don't know if you know Laura Lovell."

"Oh, yeah, the weather lady on your station?"

"Yes, that's her." Charlotte giggled. "I was thinking we could all get dinner together or something like that."

"Something like that?" Seth laughed.

"You know, go out for food sometime. Breakfast, lunch, supper, or dinner. No midnight snacks though. I get up too early every day," Charlotte giggled.

"You set it up. I'll make sure I'm there. Is Laura bringing anyone?" Seth asked.

"No, I just want it to be the three of us." Said Charlotte.

"I see." Said Seth.

"I'll let you get back to research. See you later." Said Charlotte.

"See you later," Seth put his phone back into his pocket.

Jess came back into the room, "Let me guess. That was Charlotte."

"How did you know?"

"The big grin on your face. That's how."

"She does seem to bring it out of me."

"Enjoy it! Maybe she's the one," Jess gave Seth a high five.

"I hope she is."

"Let's save this research for some other day."

"Sounds good to me. I'm heading over to Gram's place."

Lunch with Gram

Gram decided to get out her photo album. It was kept inside a huge drawer in one of her built in cabinets she had in her dining room. She opened the drawer and ran her hand over the soft blue velvet pouch the album was encased in. The album's cover was a deep brown leather. The smell of leather wafted through the air as she removed it from its pouch. She had never counted the pictures, but knew there had to be hundreds. The album was eighteen by eighteen inches. It was quite heavy. There were several different sizes of photos on the pages. The sizes ranged anywhere from 8x10 inches, 4x6 inches, 5x7 inches, and even as small as 2x2 inches. Gram took the book into the kitchen. She laid the book on the table.

At first Gram let the book remain closed for a moment. Gram bowed her head whispering, "Heavenly Father, thank you for all of these great memories."

She opened the album to the first page. There were pictures of her daughter looking up at her while being cradled in Gram's arms. Her daughter's baby pictures showed a happy baby with a big toothless grin. Her daughter's hair was dark brown. She had lots of hair. Her eyelashes were long. Her skin was dark. She had a red birthmark below her right collarbone. The birthmark was flat against her daughter's skin. The shape of the birthmark resembled a male lion's head. Its size was comparable to a coin worth twenty-five cents. Gram often called her daughter her little lion.

Gram heard a knock at the back kitchen door. She looked across the kitchen to see Seth standing outside. "Come on in Seth," Gram waved him in to come sit at the table with her.

"Hey Gram. You looking at pictures again?"

"I enjoy remembering all the good times when your mother was around."

"I do too."

"Are you hungry?"

"Yeah, a little. I was just at Jess's trying to figure out these storms that pop up out of nowhere. We have some ideas, but it's going to take a while to figure it all out," Seth sat down at the table.

Gram put the picture album back in its blue velvet pouch. She returned it to its drawer in the dining room, "Let me get my hands washed up. I'll fix you up a sandwich."

Seth nodded, "Sounds good Gram."

Gram presented Seth with a pulled roast beef sandwich with a slice of dill pickle on the side, "Here's a glass of milk to go with it. Is there anything else you may want to eat?"

Seth began biting into his sandwich, "No Gram. This is great."

Gram sat next to Seth at the table while he ate, "You mentioned the storms that pop up. They are quite strange. There was a time when those didn't happen at all."

"We'll figure it out. It is strange though. It's like they come out of nowhere, but we know there has to be something causing them," Seth began munching his pickle.

"Sometimes I wonder if it has something to do with how the weather is sometimes manipulated." Gram stated.

Seth finished up his sandwich, "I don't know about those rumors, but I know that jacking around with the weather can't be good."

Gram took Seth's plate, "It's not really any kind of rumor, Seth. Scientists started making it rain more during drought conditions so people wouldn't lose their crops. It was also a way to keep water in man-made lakes for people who live in desert areas. I'm not sure when it all began or if it has anything at all to do with what we're seeing now."

"Those seem like noble reasons to make it rain, but we still have droughts all around the world. There's still wildfires too. Whatever it is these scientists are doing must not be spot on because those problems are still here today. I'll have to brainstorm about all of this. Thanks for the food Gram. I better be on my way now. If we come up with anything, I'll let you know. It's probably going to take a while to figure all of this out."

"No worries Seth, I know you and Jess will get to the bottom of it. Tell Charlotte I said hello when you see her," Gram hugged Seth good-bye.

"I will Gram. See you soon," Seth finished hugging Gram then walked out the door.

A Relaxing Ride

It was the weekend. Charlotte was excited about going on a motorcycle ride. She liked to go on rides alone. She would spend the ride thinking about Seth. Charlotte and Seth were growing closer together each day. Seth had recovered from his long hospital stay. The two had been seeing one another several times a week for close to a year. The year went by very quickly as they created many loving memories. Charlotte was hoping that Seth would ask her to marry him.

Neither had been married to anyone else. Neither had been serious with anyone else. It didn't occur to either of them to see anyone else as they were so comfortable with one another. Charlotte changed into her black leather pants, black leather shirt, black leather jacket, and thigh high black leather boots for her journey.

She walked out to her motorcycle before the sun came up. It was inside a small garage just made for small vehicles. The motorcycle looked like something out of a science fiction film. It was metallic in color throughout the whole body. On each side of the gas tank was inscribed Matthew 5:16 in elegant golden calligraphy. Charlotte loved that verse *"Let your light so shine before men, that they may see your good works, and glorify your Father which is in heaven."*

She hopped on her motorcycle, started it up, tapped the control to close the garage door then took off into the darkness. As Charlotte rode, she thought about what a great year it had been. She remembered all of the times she sat with Seth in his truck looking at the stars and the moon. She remembered all of the times they celebrated the many storms that were wrangled.

She was even laughing to herself as she remembered conversations with Seth after he would have to save that drunken photographer Nicholas from his demise while Seth was trying to focus on the tornado coming. Seth would get so angry about that man. It made her laugh because it was unlike Seth to be angry. The look he would get on his face as he ranted about that man always made her laugh. Seth would always ask her why she was laughing. She would tell him it was the look on his face as he ranted. Seth would end up chasing her around after his rants then they'd end up entangled together rolling around on the floor or in the grass both laughing about the whole Nicholas situation.

As she rode up a winding road with tall trees on each side, she began thinking of the stories she had reported about surviving the storms. She wondered if she would always be a reporter or if it was time to look into doing something different with her life.

Charlotte was riding towards the sun as it began to rise. She could feel the warmth of the sun on her face through the visor of her motorcycle helmet. The warmth of the sun combined with thoughts of Seth made her smile. There were no other vehicles out on the road. She always loved the sense of freedom she felt being out on her bike with nobody else around.

Seth decided to check his phone to see if Charlotte had tried to call. He could see that she had left a voicemail for him. He listened to her message, He loved hearing the soprano tone in her voice when she left messages. "Hi Seth. I'm going for a ride this morning. I'll be back sometime this afternoon. I love you Seth." The message was time stamped just before dawn. Seth was used to Charlotte taking rides. He knew that he would probably see

Charlotte between two and three in the afternoon on a riding day. He would wait for her call to figure out where they'd meet later. Until then, it was time to go work out.

The Choice

Nicholas Nading was still making a living with his photographs. He had been living with Jen and Larry while his apartment complex was being rebuilt. The owners of the apartment complex had taken several months to start rebuilding it. Staying with Jen and Larry had been good for Nicholas. He didn't find himself getting fall-down drunk as much as he used to. And anytime he did get fall-down drunk, Jen would give him a piece of her mind. He respected what she had to say. The couple had been so kind to Nicholas even in his dark moments. Nicholas helped out with the bills. He was also learning how to cook. They took turns cooking dinner each week. Nicholas had thoughts of having them over to his apartment once it was finally rebuilt, so they could all stay in touch. He was hoping the couple would still invite him back for dinner from time to time.

Nicholas started expanding his portfolio with nature pictures. The storm pictures brought the most money, but people also enjoyed photos of sunsets, sunrises, and landscapes. The landscapes with animals in them were his top seller right below the storm pictures. He had a knack for action pictures. Nicholas was beginning to get famous for these pictures. People liked to have the landscape pictures with action shots made as big as a wall in their homes. The orders would pour in from all around. He would also get repeat customers who would want a new picture or they wanted to decorate several walls in their home. Some people would have the photos projected onto their walls, so they could switch scenery at any time.

Nicholas decided to go out for a drive to find some new material for his photos. He thought it might be nice to shoot some trees. He was on a winding, hilly road. There were trees all around him on each side of the road. There were maple trees, birch trees, sycamore trees, oak trees, and some pine trees. There was a parking area. He grabbed his camera gear to hike off into the forest. The trees were alive with sounds of birds, sounds of bees, and the wind was gently pushing and pulling at the tops of the trees. The leaves were rustling against each other as the wind blew through them.

Nicholas was walking slowly. As he walked, he noticed there were trees that seemed to be missing. He thought it odd then realized it was possible a Pop Up storm had hit there. Since the tornadoes of those type of storms didn't last very long, it was most likely a storm no one knew about. He was looking all around using the lens on his camera to see what type of shots he could capture here. He found branches and bark of some of the missing trees among the ones still standing. He found a good spot for his tripod. He aimed the camera straight up, straight down, and to the sides to get multiple angles of the trees that remained. Some sunlight was shimmering its way through in several spots through the canopy reaching the floor of the forest.

He decided to also get shots of the area where trees seemed to be missing. Nicholas had a really good feeling about these shots. He used many different speed settings that created different effects in the photos. After being there for a few hours, he decided it was time to take the shots back to the house. At home he could look over everything that was captured to see what photos would work best to sell.

As Nicholas was driving home, he had thought about stopping for a drink. He was thinking about having a couple of shots of whiskey somewhere. Then he began thinking about all of the photos he needed to look through. The thought of drinking left his mind. He decided to continue on home to get his work finished. It was a surprise to him that he dismissed drinking. He wasn't sure if he had ever done that before.

Nicholas got home. Larry and Jen were in the living room listening to music as he walked through the house.

"Hey Nick." Said Larry.

"Hey there Larry."

"We thought you might be out to get a drink." Said Larry.

"I thought about it." Said Nicholas. "I changed my mind. I have to get to work on these photos." Larry and Jen looked at each other surprised that Nicholas decided to skip a drink.

Nicholas was almost to his room then he turned around to go back into the living room. He looked at Larry and Jen, "I was surprised too." Nicholas quickly turned away to head back to his room.

Larry and Jen looked at one another not knowing what to say. In their joy, they hugged each other tightly.

Nicholas hooked up his camera to a monitor he had in his room to sort through the hours of photographs he had taken that day. Midnight was walking around the monitor purring and meowing for attention. Nicholas pet the cat from head to tail, "Hi there Midnight. Let's take a look and see what we captured today in the forest."

The Search Begins

It was around three thirty in the afternoon. Seth had finished his workout. He had taken a shower. He was looking through his closet to decide what to wear. It felt like a blue jean and concert shirt day. He slipped on his clothes then checked his phone. It was odd that he hadn't heard from Charlotte yet. He double checked his voicemail. There were no new messages. He thought that maybe Charlotte had decided to get a shower after her ride. He decided to check on all of his plants in his greenhouse to pass the time. Many of the plants had gotten pretty big since his stay at the hospital. Gram had been helping him take care of them, so they didn't grow out of control.

Four o'clock came. Seth still hadn't heard from Charlotte. This was unlike her. He tried to call her. The phone rang for what seemed like countless times. It finally went to voicemail. Seth left a message, "Charlotte, I haven't heard from you since this morning. It isn't like you to not call by now on a riding day. I'm heading over to your house. Call me when you get this."

Seth went out to his truck. It would take about a half an hour to get to her house. Seth wanted to get to Charlotte's more quickly than that, so put the pedal to the metal a few times to shave off some time. There weren't many people driving on the roads. He only had to pass two cars moving too slowly. Seth pulled up next to Charlotte's truck. He thought she must be home. He stood on her doorstep. He knocked on her door. He waited a minute or two and knocked again. He waited another minute. Seth decided to call her phone. He listened closely to see if he could hear the phone ringing in the house. There was nothing. It went to voicemail again.

Seth wondered if he would be able to see the motorcycle in the garage. There was a small window way up high on the side of the garage. Seth was a tall man, so was able to peek through the bottom part of the small window. The garage was empty. His heart sunk. Charlotte must be in trouble to be gone this long.

The Tornado Wranglers Weather Jacked

There was a time when Charlotte had given Seth a key to her house for emergencies if she was ever locked out. Seth remembered this. He got out his keyring. He ran back up to the front door. He opened the front door to begin looking around. Whenever Charlotte went for rides, she would keep track of them on a paper map. She would pick up a map the day before her ride at a gas station to plot her course the night before. She would take a picture of the map with her cell phone. The map had her planned course plotted out with a bright marker in case she needed to remind herself of the area she was heading to on her ride. She had shown Seth all of the maps she had used over the years. She considered the maps her souvenirs for her to keep track of all of her motorcycle rides. Seth walked into the kitchen. On the counter was the map for today's ride. He was so relieved to know that she was still using them. It would be a good starting point to look for her.

Seth decided to call Jess. With two of them looking for her, he felt like he had a better chance of finding her.

Jess's phone rang, "Hello."

"Hey Jess. I'm over at Charlotte's house. It looks like she never got back from her ride today. I was wondering if you would meet me here to help me look for her. She maps out her rides ahead of time, so I'm going to bring it with me."

"I can help. I'll get a hold of Scott to help us too. Does she have her cell with her? Maybe we could ping her cell through that pinging program."

"She always takes her cell on her rides, but she never signs up for the pinging program. That program isn't that great anyway. The cell robot teams still don't get the cell towers rebuilt quickly enough after tornadoes tear them down. She's not into people tracking her whereabouts anyway. I'll wait here at Charlotte's for you guys. "Hold on a minute. I'm getting a call." Seth got excited thinking it was Charlotte.

"Hey Seth. It's Laura. Have you heard from Charlotte today?"

Seth's heart sunk again, "No I haven't heard from her since early this morning. She went on a ride. I'm at her house right now. There's no sign of her. The motorcycle is still gone."

"I've tried calling her. It goes to voicemail. She never lets her phone go to voicemail. Maybe she's in an area where the service is bad. There's lots of bad areas." Laura replied.

"I know." said Seth. "She has it set up to ring like seven times before it goes to voicemail, so she doesn't miss any leads on the stories she works on. I have Jess on the phone too. He's going to try to get a hold of Scott. They're going to meet me here at Charlotte's. Could you come over here to stay in case she shows up here while we're gone?"

"Of course." Said Laura. "I'm on my way."

Seth switched back over to Jess, "That was Laura. I was hoping it was Charlotte. I have Laura coming over here to stay in case Charlotte comes back while we're out looking for her."

"Okay." Jess said. "I'll get a hold of Scott. We'll be over as soon as we can. Hang in there Brother. We'll find her."

Seth hung up. He studied the map of Charlotte's ride. She could be anywhere along that path.

Hopefully she didn't deviate from her planned ride he thought to himself.

Seth decided to call Gram while waiting for everyone to show up.

"Hello." Said Gram.

"Hi Gram." Said Seth.

Gram could hear in Seth's voice that something was wrong.

"Is something wrong?" Gram asked.

"Gram, if you could say a prayer for Charlotte, I think it will help. I'm going to pray too." said Seth.

"What am I praying for?" asked Gram.

"For her safe return. She went out before dawn this morning on a ride. She's not back yet. We're going to head out to look for her."

"Oh my!" said Gram. "Yes, I'll say a prayer. Let me know if there's any news."

"Thanks Gram. I will," Seth hung up.

Seth's phone was flashing. Someone must have called while he was on the line. "Oh Lord, please let it be Charlotte," Seth said aloud.

He saw there was a voicemail message. It was Charlotte's dad, "Hi Seth. I know I don't normally call you for anything. We haven't been able to reach Charlotte today. Can you give us a call?"

Seth shook his head, "Well, now I know she isn't with her parents." He let out a big sigh while calling Charlotte's dad.

Charlotte's dad answered, "Hello."

"Hey Jim. I'm at Charlotte's house right now. I haven't been here long. She went on a ride this morning. That's the last I heard from her, so I got concerned when I didn't hear from her by four this afternoon."

"I see." Said Jim.

"I have Laura coming over here to stay in case she returns. I have Jess and Scott coming over to help me look for her. I plan to take two separate vehicles." Seth explained.

"I can't sit here." Said Jim. "I will have Charlotte's mom stay here in case she stops by here. I'm heading over there now to help you guys out."

"Okay. We'll wait for you. We should have two people in each vehicle, so one can drive and the other can look around for her." Seth said.

The Tornado Wranglers Weather Jacked

Laura got to Charlotte's house. Seth was standing on the porch. She ran up to him. She hugged him.

Seth patted Laura's back as they hugged, "Don't worry Laura. We're going to find her."

"I know you will." Laura was fighting back tears as she pulled away from Seth.

Jim pulled up into the driveway at Charlotte's house. He got out of his truck. He walked up to the porch. Seth was standing there with Laura. They were looking at the map Charlotte left behind. Jim stepped next to Seth to look at the map with them. Jim was looking at the map, "She still plots her rides on these maps. That's good news."

Seth nodded his head in agreement. Scott drove into the driveway at Charlotte's. He had Jess with him. The two walked up to the porch, "What are you looking at?" asked Scott.

Seth answered, "This is our biggest clue to finding Charlotte. She maps out her rides the night before then she keeps these as a souvenir of sorts."

Scott spoke up, "I think we should put two people in each vehicle. We can take a photo of this map with our phones so we know where we're heading."

"That's what I was thinking too." Said Seth. "There are going to be dead spots as far as cell service. We should take the vehicles that have CBs in them. That way we can pick a channel to talk back and forth on. The cells just aren't as reliable as a CB out there."

"Sounds good." Said Scott. "My truck has a CB."

"So does mine." Said Seth. "Looks like we're taking those trucks then. We better head out now. She could be anywhere. Laura, we'll be back with Charlotte. We'll find her before dark hits."

"I'll be sitting here waiting." said Laura. "And praying." Laura gave Seth a quick hug. "See you all in a little while," Laura walked back into the house.

Scott and Jess got into Scott's truck. Seth and Jim got into Seth's truck. Seth got on the CB, "We need to look for tire marks on the road, drop offs in the road, drop offs on the side of the road, pay attention to the tree tops as we drive by them on these high hilly areas. If she went off the road for some reason, we should be able to see her motorcycle. It's a bright chrome color. She always wears all black leather gear when she rides for protection. If you think you see her, that's what she'll have on."

As the men drove their trucks, they looked all around them. They were even shouting Charlotte's name out of their open windows in spots where the road looked like it may give a motorcyclist trouble. They reached an area where the forest seemed thicker than other parts of the path Charlotte had plotted on her map. There was an area to pull off, so hikers could leave their cars and have easy access to the forest. Seth grabbed the CB, "Let's pull off here guys. We need to look around at this area."

"I copy that," said Scott.

All the men got out of the trucks.

Seth looked at the men, "I don't know what it is, but something led me to this area. I'm not sure why?"

Jess looked around. He saw a path that led into the woods. "It looks like this is where people go in to hike. Let's check this out first."

Seth got in front to lead the way, "Look guys, there are some tracks in here. It looks like someone was here recently." Seth knelt down to take a look at a couple of the tracks. "The prints are too big to be Charlotte's boot print. She has tiny feet."

Scott looked around, "I don't see anything that looks like motorcycle tracks either."

Jim was looking up at the trees, "We better keep looking. Inside here, it's going to be harder to see as it starts to get dark outside."

Scott brought a compass with a couple of small powerful tactical flashlights too in case darkness fell while they were out looking.

Photo Clues

Nicholas Nading was looking through all of the pictures he had taken in the forest. So far nothing was really jumping out at him that he thought would work to sell. He remembered the odd area where trees seemed to be missing. He had shot several photos of the area around it. He had seen so many storm damaged areas in his life, he couldn't count them all. He got to the pictures of the tree tops near the bare area. The tops of the trees must have been at least three stories tall by his guess. He had some pictures that zoomed in on the tops of these trees. When he was taking the pictures, he hadn't noticed anything unusual, but on his monitor at home, he saw something that looked like it was reflecting the sunlight somehow. "What is that?" he said to Midnight.

Midnight was in Nicholas's lap at this point asleep. "What would be way up there?" Nicholas clicked on the shiny object. He had read once that some birds like shiny objects. He thought maybe a bird dropped something way up there. There were so many leaves in the tree, he couldn't make out exactly what he was looking at even with zooming in on his computer. Nicholas thought that whatever it was, it was out of place. He went to get Larry and Jen to take a look with him.

Larry and Jen were still in the living room listening to music when Nicholas walked in, "I hate to interrupt. I have something in my photos that looks out of place. I was wondering if you two would take a look."

Larry and Jen both hopped up off of their couch. "We don't mind taking a look. What does it look like to you?" asked Larry.

"Whatever it is. It's shiny. There are so many leaves in the way though. I can't see exactly what it is." Said Nicholas.

Jen and Larry walked into Nicholas's room. The monitor was twenty-four inches, so was easy to see the full picture.

Nicholas walked up to the monitor. He took his finger drawing a circle around the part of the photo in question.

"That's shiny alright." Said Jen. "Do you have different angles of this?"

Nicholas clicked on more pictures, "I was moving the tripod around as I shot these. Let me flip forward a few more minutes. It was just so odd looking to me, I hadn't looked at the rest of these close up yet."

"Stop right there." Said Jen. "Zoom in a little more in this area," Jen made a circle with her finger on the image on the screen.

Nicholas wasn't sure what he what seeing. "What is it?"

Jen took her finger and started making circles in different areas of the leaves of the tree. "I'm seeing all kinds of shiny things. This looks like one big object to me. How tall are these trees?"

Nicholas looked at Jen, "I'm guessing they're at least three stories tall, but I really don't know."

Larry looked concerned, "It's really hard to tell with the leaves what exactly we're looking at here. Was it windy at all?"

Nicholas thought about it for a second or two, "Yes, it was breezy. The leaves were rustling against each other in the wind. I didn't take any video. I'm going to have to go frame by frame for several minutes to see if we can piece this together."

"Maybe if you click through the pictures a little faster, we can put the image together a little easier." Said Jen.

"I'll try it, but I'm not sure if it will help." Said Nicholas.

"It would be like watching a video if we do that. It could bring it into focus for us." Replied Jen. Nicholas erased all the circles they had made. He drew a box around the area to focus on. The three of them watched as he clicked through the photos quickly.

After the seventh time of flipping through the sequence of pictures, Jen had put it together, "I think it's some kind of vehicle in the tree, Nick. Maybe it got carried there in a storm at some point. That kind of tree looks like a strong oak. There's no telling how long it's been up there."

Nicholas could kind of see what Jen was saying. "You think it's a car?"

Jen shook her head, "I think we're either seeing part of a car or some other kind of vehicle. Maybe nobody ever spotted it before just because they weren't looking up. They were looking down at the path while hiking. You were purposely looking up, but your camera caught it with its telephoto lens."

Larry circled a part of the screen with his finger, "We're seeing many little shiny parts through here. I wonder why it's still so shiny if it's been up there awhile. You would think with dust flying through the air, birds, and other animals that live in the trees, it would be dirtier whatever it is."

Nicholas raised his bright red eyebrows, "Unless, the vehicle hasn't been up in the tree very long. You know, it was strange because this was near an area that looked like trees were missing.

You can see back here in these pictures what I'm talking about." Nicholas clicked back to show them the bare area.

Larry frowned, "It could have been a Pop Up storm. Is that what you're saying? It ripped a few trees out of the ground then picked up whatever we're seeing in this tree?"

Nicholas nodded his head, "This isn't good. There's been so many of those in the past few months that disappear before the wranglers can get to them. They must not have known about it. I noticed the trees gone, but I didn't notice this shiny stuff until I brought the pictures up on the computer here."

Jen looked at Larry and Nicholas, "There could be someone up in that tree."

Nicholas shook his head, "Let's hope not. I have to report this right away. I had no idea earlier today. It's getting dark outside. I don't think anyone will be able to do anything about it tonight."

Larry shook his head, "Nick, let me report it. Let's face it, you have caused the wranglers lots of trouble over the years chasing down your storm photos. I'll take care of it. They may think you're just trying to cause them more trouble."

Nicholas hung his head, "You're right. I can't think of a time I dealt with them when I was completely sober."

Jen turned to Larry, "I still keep the number on the fridge next to our landline phone if you want to call them now."

Larry nodded, "Yeah, I better get them the information tonight, so they can go take a look at sunrise. They'll probably need a drone crane and the State Guard to help them."

Lingering Hope

Laura was sitting in a wing chair at Charlotte's house. It was dark outside. She turned the outside lights on for the guys. Just about that time, she saw headlights coming towards the house. It looked like Seth and the guys. Laura ran out to the driveway expecting to see Charlotte.

Everyone got out of the trucks.

Laura looked around, "Where's Charlotte?"

Seth shook his head, "Laura, we didn't find her."

"Did you see her motorcycle anywhere?" asked Laura. All of the men shook their heads.

Seth walked up onto the porch and turned to face everyone in the driveway, "It's late. We need to try to sleep until the sun comes up. We can look again in the morning. I think we should all meet back at the same spot. For some reason, I couldn't shake the feeling that Charlotte might be in that area. I just don't know where."

Jim walked up onto the porch too, "By tomorrow, Charlotte is considered a missing person. We don't know what happened. I'm setting my alarm for sunrise. If none of us have heard from her by then, I'm going to report her missing to the police. Many people have seen her on the news. I'm sure her viewers will want to help. I'll call her news station tomorrow too."

"I'm staying put." Said Laura. "If she shows up here tonight, I'll call all of you even if it's one in the morning."

Jim walked back to his truck. He got inside to call his wife, "Hello, Sarah."

Sarah could tell Jim was sad. "Is Charlotte with you, Jim?"

Jim sighed, "No. No, she's not."

"What happened?" Sarah asked.

"Sarah, we don't know. We can't find her. Seth thinks she is in this wooded area. He said he had a feeling about it. We looked for her until it got dark. We yelled for her. There was no sign of her."

"No sign at all?" asked Sarah. "Not even her motorcycle?"

"Not even that. If we haven't heard from her by sunrise, I'm going to call the police. I'll call her news station as well." Said Jim.

Seth got in his truck to head back to his house. He didn't know how he was going to sleep knowing Charlotte was not home. He knew he needed the rest though for a fresh start in the morning.

Once Seth got home, he took a hot shower. He couldn't shake the feeling that Charlotte might be in that wooded area somewhere. It got dark so quickly. If only they had more time to search. After his shower, he went to his bed. He lifted up his sheets to lie down. The sheets smelled of clean detergent as they floated down onto his body. He looked at his phone to check for messages one last time. There was a voicemail. His heart beat fast hoping it was Charlotte.

Disappointed again, it was from Sherry. Sherry didn't even know Charlotte was missing. He figured he better listen to it in case it had something to do with storms coming, "Hi Seth. Sherry here. I got a weird call tonight. This guy said that there was some kind of vehicle way up high in a tree. He was worried it might be from a Pop Up storm that nobody knew about. He was also worried somebody might be inside the vehicle way up in the tree.

He said that there were trees near it that had disappeared. It looked like they were pulled out of the ground. I know we usually handle things as they're happening. I don't know what you want to do about it, but you can't do anything until it's light out anyway. The guy's name is Larry."

Seth was more tired than he thought. He fell asleep immediately after listening to Sherry's message. In his dreams, he was walking all over the woods looking for Charlotte. He found her in a clearing standing in the sunshine. Her helmet was sitting on the ground. She saw Seth walking up to her. Before he could say anything to her, she tackled him to the ground giggling all the way down. Seth woke up laughing. It hit him that it was just a dream. He was sad again. He looked over at the time. The sun would be up soon.

Laura's phone was buzzing and jingling. She picked it up to hear Jim on the other end, "Have you heard from Charlotte?"

"No, I haven't. I barely slept. I kept checking my phone. There's nothing. I'm sorry." Said Laura.

Jim let out a big sigh, "I'm going to make the calls then."

The Climb

Seth was at the forest waiting for the others to arrive. The sun wasn't up yet. He was sitting in his truck. He had his radio playing low. An announcer came on, "We have breaking news. Charlotte Coles who is a reporter for our local TV station has been reported as missing. If you have seen Charlotte, please call us. She was last known to be riding her motorcycle. The motorcycle is all chrome colored. It has the words Matthew 5:16 inscribed on the gas tank known to friends and family as one of her favorite Holy Bible verses. Charlotte was wearing black leather pants, a jacket, boots, and a helmet. Please tune into the local news for further details on the disappearance of Charlotte Coles." Seth turned off the radio hanging his head. He heard a tap at his truck window. He looked over to find Nicholas Nading standing there. Seth rolled down his window, "What do YOU want? Don't you give me enough trouble?"

Nicholas blurted out, "Yeah, yeah. I know I had lots of drunken run-ins with you while you guys were trying to wrangle tornadoes. I thought you were here because of the call you got from Larry."

Seth looked surprised, "Larry? How did you know about Larry?"

Nicholas explained, "He's a friend of mine."

Seth shook his head. Seth thought Nicholas was playing a game, "I didn't think you had any friends. Wait a minute. I don't smell alcohol on you. What's going on here?"

Nicholas put up his hands, "There's really no time to go into details. There's a tree with a vehicle in it in there. It's so high up, it's hard to tell if there's anyone inside."

Suddenly Seth realized that the call he got from Sherry was about the woods he was sitting in front of. "These woods? There's a vehicle up in a tree here?"

"Yes. Inside there," Nicholas pointed into the woods.

"What kind of vehicle?" asked Seth.

Nicholas shrugged, "I don't know. I can't tell from the pictures. I was shooting pictures, lots of pictures. You can just see pieces, but it has to be a vehicle."

"Can you tell what color it is in the pictures?" asked Seth.

"Yeah, it's shiny like chrome." Nicholas answered.

Seth jumped out of his truck. He grabbed Nicholas by his shoulders pulling him closer, "This better not be one of your stunts, Nicholas."

Jess pulled up just in time to see Seth grab Nicholas by the shoulders. Jess got out of his truck rushing over to the men, "What are you doing here, Nicholas?"

Nicholas stepped back removing Seth's hands from his shoulders, "I saw something up in a tree in there. I thought you guys were coming to check it out. That's all."

Seth looked at Jess, "I don't think he knows about Charlotte."

Nicholas frowned, "What about Charlotte?"

"She's missing." Said Jess somberly.

Nicholas looked surprised. "I had no idea! I've been busy with all of these pictures. I didn't know anything about it. Sorry guys. Really."

The three men were looking at the ground. Jess looked up at Nicholas, "You don't smell like alcohol." Jess moved closer to Nicholas. "All I smell is coffee on your breath." Jess was confused.

Nicholas nodded his head, "Yeah, I haven't been drinking. Look guys, the sun is starting to come up. I can show you that tree I came across in my pictures."

Charlotte's dad pulled up then Scott pulled up. The two men walked over to Seth, Jess and Nicholas.

Scott looked at Nicholas, "What in the world are YOU doing here?"

"There's no time to explain now, just follow me," said Nicholas.

Charlotte's dad and Scott looked to Seth for confirmation, "It's okay guys, let's follow him. I think this time, he won't cause us trouble."

Nicholas led the way followed by Seth, Jim, Jess, and Scott brought up the back of the group. The men came to an area where it looked like trees had been pulled up. Nicholas turned around to speak to the men, "This is where I shot a bunch of pictures. If you look up to the East, you can see some tree tops. See that tree with the broken branches all around? Near the top is a shape in my shots that looks like a vehicle." All the men looked up, but couldn't see anything.

Jim spoke up, "I don't see anything up there."

"That's just it," said Nicholas. "You can't see it from way down here. It's just too high. There's no telling how long it's been up there."

Seth looked to Scott, "Did you bring climbing gear?"

"As a matter of fact, I did," said Scott. "I thought I may have to climb a tree for a different perspective. Scott opened a backpack that had special shoes in it for climbing trees. The shoes had spiky steel horns on the bottoms for a good grip on the bark of the trees. He also had rope so he could rappel back down instead of climbing down. "Been climbing everything my whole life including trees."

"That tree is at least eighty or ninety feet tall. Maybe even more. You sure you want to climb it?" asked Jim.

"Doesn't bother me any." Said Scott. He was working to get the shoes put on his feet to begin his climb. "If I can get close to the vehicle, I should be able to see if anyone is inside it." Scott started to climb the tree.

Seth stopped him, "Scott, Nicholas said the color was shiny like chrome. It might be Charlotte's motorcycle."

"If it is her motorcycle, she may be with it. Only way to find out is to go look. Here goes." Scott continued climbing. Scott had a small high tech walkie talkie clipped to the top of his vest.

Seth had the other walkie talkie to keep in touch with him as Scott climbed higher out of view. Scott began speaking to Seth through the walkie talkie, "I can see the bottom of the vehicle now. It is way up here. It had to be a tornado that brought it up here. No doubt about that. The way it's stuck in the tree is almost like the tree reached out and grabbed it. I'm going to attempt to climb around it to get more above it. I hope it doesn't jar loose. You guys down there need to move back. If you hear anything and I mean anything, run."

"No problem," said Seth. "Be safe Scott."

"Here goes nothing," said Scott. "I'm moving up right next to it. It's definitely a motorcycle. Let me get just a little higher here." Scott positioned himself where he could plainly see the motorcycle sitting in the tree. At this point, his breathing was labored. It had been a long climb.

Sweat was pouring from his forehead down into his eyes. "Hold on a second. I need to try to wipe this sweat out of my eyes." Scott wiped his eyes on his shirt sleeves to get a better look at the motorcycle through the foliage of the tree, "I can't see the gas tank. There are a few little branches covering it. Let me rig up my rappelling rope, so I can get to those little branches." He rigged up his rope getting closer to the gas tank of the motorcycle, "Look out below, I'm going to snap these tiny branches out of the way." The men down below moved way back. They could hear the snapped off branches falling to the ground as they hit other tree branches on their way.

"Okay, yeah. This is definitely Charlotte's motorcycle. I'm looking all around. There's no sign of Charlotte anywhere up here guys. I'm sorry."

Seth's heart sunk. It was a reminder of when he was a child when there was a massive search for his mother. It took a long time to find her, but they didn't find her alive. "We wish you had better news, but at least we know what happened now. We can get a drone crane in here to get her motorcycle down. We'll have to do a massive search. Charlotte could be anywhere."

Jim walked over to Seth, "I'll let the news station and police know what we found. If we can get as many people as possible aware, we'll have a better chance of finding her. For now, I think we should keep scanning this area. A dog would be good to have too. A dog may be able to pick up her scent."

Nicholas was standing next to Seth, "I'll give David and Lucy a call. Lucy should be able to sniff Charlotte out."

Scott landed safely on the ground. He unhooked himself from his gear. He walked over to Seth., "Keep the faith, Seth. We'll find her."

Out of nowhere, the tornado sirens started wailing. The wind was whipping the CB antennas all around on the trucks. Sherry's voice was coming over the CB, "Seth we got a tornado on the ground. Repeat. We got a tornado on the ground. I'm coming to pick you guys up! E.T.A. two minutes." Sherry heard nothing back from the guys.

The Fall

The tops of the trees were bending with every howl of the winds. The men heard loud cracking sounds. Scott shouted over the winds, "Dive for that ditch over there! The motorcycle is coming down at us!" The men ran then jumped into the ditch. The motorcycle broke several branches on its way down. Branches and leaves were flipping through the winds. Charlotte's motorcycle tumbled end over end until it hit the forest floor landing on its side. As quickly as the winds inflicted their damage, they suddenly stopped. There was complete silence.

All the men were hunkered down in the ditch. Nicholas spoke up in the silence, "Well, this isn't good." Just about that time, a tornado swept over the top of the ditch. It didn't touch down, but debris was flying everywhere. The men protected their heads as best they could with their arms and their faces were pressed against the soil of the earth. The tornado only lasted about twenty seconds in their area, but it felt like time had stopped as it moved overhead. Every stick, twig, leaf, bug, bird, and squirrel that found itself flying over the ditch seemed to almost float in slow motion.

The Tornado Wranglers Weather Jacked

It felt like the storm had passed, so the men began climbing out of the ditch giving each other a hand pulling one another up. Jim was the last to be pulled out. As he stepped forward to reach up the toe of his boot hit something, "Wait a minute," Jim said to Seth. "I feel something odd under the toe of my shoe here. Let me take a look," Jim bent down to look. The object he saw was covered with mud and sticks. Underneath he found a helmet. He picked it up. On the sides were painted golden angel wings. "Guys, I just found my daughter's helmet." He looked inside the helmet. A clump of Charlotte's long red hair was stuck to the foam inside. The foam was soaked in blood. "Something or someone ripped this off her head," Jim began shaking his head wondering what had happened to his daughter. He held up the helmet to show the others.

Seth didn't want to give up on Charlotte, "We're going to ask Charlotte what happened when we find her," Seth extended his hand down to Jim to help him up.

Jess looked at the men, "We don't need the drone crane now. We better go take a look at the motorcycle. She may have left clues behind there."

The men walked over to the motorcycle. Seth began checking the storage compartments, "I'm hoping her phone isn't in here. If she had it in her jacket, it may still be on her." One storage compartment was jammed. "So far so good. If I could just get this last one opened," Seth grunted a little digging his fingers into the compartment door trying to pry it open. The compartment door sprung open. A banana rolled out onto the ground. Seth let out a laugh, "I'm so glad her phone isn't in here!" The other men let out laughs of relief as well.

Jess was still laughing, "A banana isn't much of a clue, but much better than finding her phone. Did she ever turn off her phone for any reason?"

Seth thought for a minute. "Yeah, she may have turned it off to save the battery life."

Jim shook his head, "Maybe, but she's been missing a long time. You would think she would have turned it back on by now to call someone."

Jess considered that, "Or she could be in an area where there's no cell service."

Seth nodded his head, "I thought about that too."

Sherry reached the area where the men had parked their trucks. She could see that a storm had blown through. It wasn't the tornado she had tracked in the TSV. As she walked up to Seth's truck, she could hear the men walking towards her and talking. As they came out of the woods, Sherry hollered over to them, "Hey guys. We had a tornado to wrangle, but it's already gone. Tried to reach you on the CB. Were you looking for that car in the tree?"

Seth led the group over to Sherry, "Sorry. We were in the woods. The radar looked clear today. It was Charlotte's motorcycle."

Sherry looked surprised, "What? Where's Charlotte?"

Seth shook his head, "We don't know. She's missing. Everyone has been looking for her including the police."

Sherry's eyes got really wide, "I had no idea. I'm so sorry to hear that." She threw her arms around Seth to hug him.

Jess walked over to Sherry, "You were asleep when I got back to headquarters. You were still asleep this morning when I left. The sun wasn't up yet."

Jim had cleaned off Charlotte's helmet as best he could while walking back to the trucks, "We found her helmet too," he held it up so Sherry could see it. "Charlotte's news station is showing her picture. The radio has been letting people know too."

Nicholas spoke up, "We should keep that helmet handy for Lucy to sniff. If Charlotte is anywhere around here, Lucy will find her."

Jess looked over at Nicholas, "Do you know when they're coming?"

"I'm waiting to hear back. If they're on any other case right now, it may not be today." Answered Nicholas.

Seth pulled away from Sherry to get his cell phone, "Nicholas, I'm going to give you my cell so you can let me know when Lucy is coming." Seth pushed a button on his cell then tapped it against the phone Nicholas had.

"Okay, I see it in my contacts now," said Nicholas. "I'll get a hold of you as soon as I know."

Sherry started walking back to the TSV, "I'm going to head back to headquarters in case any other tornadoes show up. I need to find out what happened with the one we missed too. We may not have gotten to it in time anyway. They come and go so quickly sometimes."

Jess looked at Sherry, "I better head back too in case another tornado comes. These guys can keep looking for Charlotte."

The men started yelling Charlotte's name as loud as they could after Sherry and Jess drove away. Then they would stay silent to listen. No response. They yelled again in unison as loud as they could. They listened again. Nothing. Seth looked at everyone, "Let's yell one last time really loud!" They gave one last yell in unison, "Charlotte!" Then they all listened again. Still no response.

Jim spoke up, "We should be hearing a chopper looking for her any time now. I gave the police a copy of her map. They may have better luck in the air."

Seth looked hopeful, "That's how they found my mom. Let's split up again. We can take the trucks out until dark. Maybe we missed something."

Mystery Call

Laura Lovell was back at Charlotte's house hoping for Charlotte's return. She had the television on in the background watching for any updates. She hadn't heard from Seth, so didn't know if he had found anything. Laura was still checking her phone every few minutes thinking Charlotte may call. Another day had gone by. It was dark again. She heard someone pull up in the gravel driveway. It was Seth. She hurried out onto the porch. Seth was walking up to meet her. "Did you find her?" Laura asked.

Seth rubbed his eyes as he shook his head no. They sat down on the porch step together staring at the ground. Seth let out a big sigh, "You know, I waited too long."

Laura turned her head to Seth, "What do you mean?"

"I've been with Charlotte for close to a year now. I have a ring sitting at home in this tiny box. I had planned to propose to her. Jess was going to set off some fireworks for me if she said yes. I wanted it to be special because she is the one. I guess I waited too long."

Laura punched Seth in the arm, "You're giving up! Don't give up!"

Seth rubbed his arm, "You punch pretty hard woman! You're right. I shouldn't give up. On the way here I was just thinking of how long it took to find my mom. When we did find her, it was too late. I think it's all just getting to me because of that. They brought a chopper out to look. They didn't see her. I was positive the chopper would be our answer."

"Maybe she's in a spot the chopper can't see? What's the next step then?" Laura leaned her head on Seth's shoulder as she looked at the ground.

"I stopped here to update you. I thought I'd try to eat something too. We're all meeting David and Lucy tomorrow to see if Lucy can sniff her out," Seth was still staring at the ground.

Laura moved her feet back and forth over the gravel, "Did you find anything promising?"

Seth sighed, "What we found isn't good."

Laura sighed, "I still want to know."

"Her motorcycle was way up high in a tree almost the very top of it. You couldn't even tell from the ground. Then Jim found her helmet in a ditch."

"Well, that seems like good news to me," Laura got excited hopping up to stand in front of Seth.

"Laura, the problem is that the helmet had some of her hair in it. Not just a little hair, but a clump of hair. The inside of the helmet…was bloody. We don't know how it got that way without talking to Charlotte." Seth got a knot in his throat at the thought of Charlotte's blood. It was difficult to speak, "Sooo, if Lucy can sniff her out, I don't know exactly what we're going to find."

Laura began to cry, "Oh! I understand now." Seth stood up pulling her up into his shoulder. She was crying so hard, tears were soaking through his shirt. He held her patting her back softly for a few minutes letting her get it all out. She pulled back wiping away tears streaming down her cheeks with the backs of both of her hands, "I was fine until you told me about the blood," she sniffled as she wiped the backs of her hands on the back of her jeans.

Seth wrapped one arm around Laura's side. They walked slowly into the house, "Let's get you cleaned up. There's still a chance that she's fine. I didn't want to upset you, but you wanted to know."

They walked into Charlotte's bathroom. Seth sat on the side of the tub while Laura splashed water on her face. "I'm using ice cold water. I need to wake up. I've barely slept."

"I know what you're saying. Same here." Seth replied. "I need to try to eat something. I haven't felt like eating. The two walked into the kitchen. Laura opened the fridge, "I made some tuna salad earlier. There's still some left. Do you want that?"

"Yeah, I'll split a sandwich with you. That's probably all I can eat." Seth answered.

Laura prepared a sandwich cutting it in half, "I'll eat my half later. Do you want milk or mineral water to drink?"

"Milk sounds okay," Seth took a small bite of the sandwich.

Laura's phone began ringing and buzzing. She had left it on the side table in the living room. The lights all around the perimeter of the phone were flashing. She ran into the living room to see who it was. Charlotte's number with her picture was flashing on the screen. Laura's heart started racing and thumping. She picked up the phone, "Charlotte!" She listened, but there was nothing.

"Charlotte! Is it you? Where are you?" She waited for a reply.

All Laura heard was a whisper, "Help."

Seth ran in to see what was happening, "Did she say anything?"

"I have to try to call her back. She whispered help." Laura called Charlotte back right away. It rang and rang and rang and rang. It finally went to voice mail. "She's not answering!" It was so frustrating!

Seth took the phone from Laura, "Slow down. Tell me what happened."

"She wasn't answering me. When I asked her where she was, she whispered help then it went dead."

"Let's sit down to think about this," Seth sat down on the couch with Laura next to him. He sat there silently looking at Laura's phone, "We definitely know it was her phone. We both know that Charlotte has your phone number on there as the first one to call since you're her best friend. We also know that

Charlotte doesn't need to punch in a code or anything to use her phone. She hates that code stuff. I hope it was her and not someone who found her phone. You said you heard a whisper?"

Laura nodded her head, "Yeah, it was definitely the word help. It was like the phone wasn't up to her mouth or like she was out of breath. You said there was blood in her helmet. She would text me if she could. We have to find her!"

Seth handed the phone back to Laura, "David and Lucy will be at the forest at sunrise. I'm going to let everyone know she called. She may try to call back again. This gives us hope, Laura."

Seth went back to his truck to head home. As he was pulling out, Laura came running out of the house with his sandwich and milk. Laura ran up to the driver's side window, "Here Seth, eat this on the way home."

Seth took the sandwich placing the milk glass in his cup holder, "Thanks Laura. I totally forgot about my food." Seth pulled away while taking bites of his sandwich. He could see Laura in his rear view mirror standing under the security light. There was dust whipping around her from the gravel driveway.

As soon as Seth got home, he called Jim, "Laura got a call from Charlotte."

"What?" asked Jim.

"Charlotte called Laura."

Jim got excited, "What did she say? Is she okay?"

"All Laura could hear was the word help. It was a whisper or like when you're out of breath."

"Oh," Jim replied. "Did Laura call her back?"

Seth was pacing his house while talking with Jim, "She tried calling her back, but it rang and rang. The thing is, we don't know if it was her. She doesn't use a code or anything for her phone, so it could be someone who has her phone. The fact that there was just a whisper though makes us think it was really her. Her helmet makes it look like she's hurt pretty bad. She may be in and out of consciousness for all we know."

Jim was sitting outside in the dark listening to Seth. He now had hope his daughter was still hanging on, "We'll meet you at sunrise as planned. I'll let the police know about the call. Try to sleep if you can."

"We have hope now Jim. She's hanging on. See you in a few hours," Seth hung up.

Lucy to the Rescue

The men met back at the forest at sunrise as planned. Jess stayed at headquarters in case a tornado needed wrangled.

David and Lucy were standing in front of the group, "If anyone can find Charlotte, Lucy can."

The Tornado Wranglers Weather Jacked

Jim handed the helmet to David, "Here's Charlotte's helmet."

David put the helmet up to Lucy's face. She put one paw upon the helmet. It was her way of asking David to put the helmet on the ground for her. David put it on the ground. Lucy had her face down inside the helmet sniffing and sniffing. Then she sniffed the outside of it as well. David had Lucy fastened to her red leash. Once she was through sniffing, she jumped forward with her tail straight out pulling her leash taught, "She's ready to find her now. Go find Charlotte, Lucy. Go find her, girl," David unhooked the leash. Lucy took off up the path towards the ditch. Everyone was walking as fast as they could to keep up with her.

Nicholas brought up the back of the group yelling up to the front almost out of breath, "At this fast pace, we should find her pretty quickly guys!"

David yelled back, "Letting her off the leash helps her move more quickly that's for sure. Once she finds Charlotte, she'll signal us with barks." Right about the time David said that, he lost sight of Lucy. This happened often during searches. "I just lost sight of her guys, but don't worry if we can't tell where she went, I can whistle for her. She'll come back to lead us to Charlotte." David could hear that a couple of the men were breathing hard trying to keep up. "Let's stop a minute guys. We'll rest a minute to catch our breath. I can still hear Lucy walking."

Jim stopped while putting his hands on his knees to rest, "I won't argue with resting a minute. I haven't slept much or eaten much. I can hear the dog walking too."

Seth looked at Jim, "I plan to bring Charlotte home today."

A Glimpse of Reality

Something wet was moving under the left side of Charlotte's head. It felt cold too. She realized that she had been sleeping on her side, but why? She wondered why she wasn't on her stomach. That's how she usually slept.

She couldn't feel her left arm like it was asleep. Something was poking into her left leg. She tried to move, but she was stuck in something. The back of her head was stinging as something flowed over it. She heard a strange noise that sort of sounded like a dog drinking water. She tried opening her eyes to look around her. Her beautiful big brown eyes were now swollen almost completely shut. She managed to open her eyes just slightly into little slits. What she saw startled her. There was a doe's mouth in the water lapping a drink right next to her face.

The realization hit that she was lying in a body of a water. The water wasn't deep. The poking sensation in her left leg was a bed of rocks below the water line. She tried to speak. All that happened was a tiny puff of air came out of her lips. Oh God, please let this be a nightmare not my reality, she thought. Her breaths felt short like she couldn't get enough air. She tried to move her right leg. It flopped in front of her left leg into the water. The doe didn't like the splash, so high tailed it into the woods. She had no idea where she was and was trying to remember how she got there.

The last memory she had was being on her motorcycle. She could feel her helmet was missing. Her hair was floating back and forth in the water. If she could open her eyes more maybe she could figure out where she was. She wished she could sit up, but it seemed impossible. It was like her mind and body weren't one anymore.

She looked around as best she could. She could move her head, but when she did, there was intense pain that would shoot from the back of her head to the front of her head then into her eyes. She scanned the water near her head. She could feel something resting in her right hand. It was her cell phone. Her hand was holding it as if she had made a call. There was water rushing over her hand. As she tried to lift her hand to see her phone, everything she could see turned pitch dark. She heard a high pitched tone in her left ear. Her right arm dropped like dead weight into the water. A wave of water from her arm smacking down into the creek overtook her phone. The phone floated downstream for at least a half mile until it got wedged between two slate rocks on the side of the creek. Water was rushing all around the two rocks where the phone was resting. Charlotte's body was still, her eyes totally closed now, and her red hair was still floating from side to side in the cool water.

Cell Phone Nightmare

Laura was keeping busy at Charlotte's. She vacuumed, dusted, cleaned the bathroom, and even washed the windows on the front door. It's not that Charlotte's house needed to be cleaned. Laura just needed something to do besides stare at her phone waiting for it to ring again. The news had been running Charlotte's picture every chance it got hoping someone somewhere had seen her in the local area. The police were always led to a dead end.

Laura's phone began ringing and buzzing. It was Charlotte again. Laura's heart started pounding in her chest, "Hello!" There was no hello in return. "Charlotte, are you there?" There was nothing but noise. Laura listened intently to the phone. She heard what reminded her of water running in the bathtub. The call wasn't disconnecting. She turned up the volume on her phone to see if she could make out any other sounds. There was something making noise behind the sounds of the water. It sounded like birds chirping in the trees. The call disconnected. Laura tried to call Charlotte back. This time a three toned buzzing came through then a robotic sounding woman's voice said, "We're sorry. The number you dialed cannot be reached at this time. Try your call again later."

That made Laura pretty angry, "Stupid, stupid, stupid cell phones!" She frantically called back again. Again, she heard, "We're sorry." Laura hung up and began to cry. At this point she was on her knees down on the floor, "Please God, help us find her. Please help us God." Then Laura came to realize that she needed to get a hold of Seth. Charlotte must be near water.

The Howl

"I can't hear Lucy anymore," said David. "I think she stopped." Lucy began barking. "This way guys," David started walking faster. Lucy continued barking to signal she had found something.

"We'll catch up to her. I'm going to move just a little faster guys. Let's go." He picked up the pace even faster to try to get to Lucy, "Don't be alarmed guys. She is trained to bark until I get there. And if I don't get there fast enough, she comes to me. The only problem is she has four legs and I only have two. Takes me longer."

Seth's legs were strong. He wasn't feeling anything but hope as they trudged closer and closer to Lucy. He kept picturing Charlotte's face in his mind the closer they got. He couldn't wait to see her again. Seth made a declaration, "When I find out who's been jacking with the weather, they're going to pay. They caused this. I know they did."

Nicholas thought to himself, "What is Seth talking about? Weather is weather." He decided not to say anything.

Jim was having trouble keeping up again, but managed to blurt out breathlessly, "I don't know what you're talking about. Let's bring my daughter home."

Scott never talked much during the trudge. He knew exactly what Seth was talking about, but stayed silent.

Lucy began to howl. David stopped. He looked back at the guys, "She's never done that before. Since we don't know where she is exactly, I'm going to whistle for her. She'll come to me then lead us to where she's howling."

Seth looked at David, "What do you mean she's never done that before?"

David said, "Just that. She's never howled when she's found someone. It's always barking not howling. I don't want to take the chance that we're walking in the wrong direction to get to her. I'll use the dog whistle, Lucy will get to us as fast as she can then lead us to Charlotte. Sometimes out here in the woods, you think a sound is coming from one direction when it's not. I don't want to take a chance on this. Let's wait here for her." David began blowing on the whistle. The howling stopped. The men could hear the dog running through the woods to get to them. "Hear her running? Let's rest a minute while we wait."

The Tornado Wranglers Weather Jacked

Seth decided to check his phone while they waited. He knew the signal was low here, but thought he would check it anyway, "Hey guys, I have a text here from Laura. It looks like she sent it about an hour ago. My phone must have just picked it up. She got another call from Charlotte! She could hear water and birds. She's probably by some water. It's good news! We're bringing her home. I just know it!" Seth was ecstatic.

Scott high fived Seth, "You know it Seth!"

David looked at Seth, "Lucy will find her. Here she comes now. Let's go guys."

Lucy's tongue was hanging out. The run back to the men had made her hot. David hooked up her red leash to her. Lucy walked fast keeping the leash taught as she led the men to where she had been howling. They came to an area where the terrain went upward. There was no trail. It was somewhat steep as well. The men had to use their hands as they climbed up to reach the top.

Once they got to the top, Lucy started barking. David looked to the group of men, "I'm going to let her go now. I think we're close." Lucy ran off, but was still within eyesight. She stopped at a stream. She began drinking the water.

Seth saw that she was drinking, "Lucy was just thirsty. Look, she needed a drink."

Lucy stopped lapping up the water, got into the water, stepped forward a few feet, sat down then started howling again.

David was confused, "Why is she howling? I'm sorry guys, I don't know what she's doing." The group of men caught up to the dog at this point. David walked up to the edge of the water. The dog was still howling. "Lucy, stop!" David commanded. The dog refused. "Okay girl, do you see something? What do you see?" Lucy stopped howling then pawed at some slate rocks in the creek.

Seth looked at David, "What is she doing? Playing in the water now?" Seth's stomach was in knots. He had expected to see Charlotte here.

David shrugged, "Let me take a look over here. I think she's trying to show us something." He walked into the stream, "Guys, there's something here."

Seth walked into the water next to David, "What is it?"

David was trying to move a heavy, flat, slab of rock, "There is something wedged in here between these slabs of rock. I can't tell what it is for sure. Let me push this just a little harder this way." The rock splashed to the side releasing the object. David grabbed it up, "It's a phone!" He held it up so everyone could see. Lucy had walked back up to rest on the side of the stream.

"Good job Lucy! Good job girl!"

Lucy barked back twice as if to say thank you.

David handed the phone to Seth. Seth took a look at the phone, "This is definitely Charlotte's. The back of the phone is inscribed with her initials CC here at the top corner. Then down here along the bottom is inscribed Revelation 20:12. That's another Holy Bible verse she likes to remember. She had all of this put on there in case she ever misplaced it. I wonder where Charlotte is. I remember when I was a kid, my mom was a whole town away when we found her," Seth's stomach turned as he spoke that aloud.

Jim had found a rock to sit on, "I'm not going to believe she is in another town. We need to keep searching. The police have followed all the clues the public has given them. They haven't found her yet. She has to be up here. David, you said that Lucy had never howled like that before. What do you think it means?"

David walked over to Lucy to give her some food he was carrying on him, "I'm not sure if it's because she found the phone instead of Charlotte or what? I'll have her sniff the phone to pick up the scent again and we'll keep moving."

Jim stood up, "That's a plan."

Nicholas had been leaning against a tree to rest, "We'll find her. I have no doubt."

Scott had brought a few things in his medical backpack in case it was necessary when they found Charlotte. He readjusted it on his back nodding his head in agreement to continue.

Lucy sniffed the phone in David's hand. He repositioned it a few times so she could get a good whiff of Charlotte's scent again. He clipped the red leash to her once again as she led the way.

She led them through the shallow water.

Scott yelled up to David, "How is she smelling anything in this?"

David yelled back, "I think the phone must have hit lots of rocks as it was floating. She's picking up the scent off that. This is a really rocky creek." Suddenly Lucy jerked the leash really hard.

David's hand wasn't ready for that, "Okay girl, I'll let you go." David rubbed his hand that was writhing in pain. The K9 ran full blast ahead. Suddenly she stopped. She started howling again. All the men began running to see what was happening.

Seth moved in front of David like greased lightning leaving everyone else behind. When he was about ten feet away from the howling dog, he saw a motionless body in the water. Seth began yelling, "Charlotte! Charlotte!" as he ran up to her body. He started stomping around in the water crying and yelling, "Please God! Noooooo! She's dead! She's dead! Please God! Nooooooo!"

Scott pushed Seth out of the way, "Somebody take him away from her!"

Nicholas grabbed Seth from behind by his arms pulling him back with all his might.

Jim stood back with tears streaming down his face. The only way he could recognize his daughter was her long red hair flowing back and forth in the water. Her face and neck was so purple from bruising. There was nothing left of her beautiful skin to be seen from her forehead clear down to her collar bone. Her leather motorcycle outfit had rips and tears in various places.

Lucy walked over to Jim whining. Jim began petting the dog as he looked at Charlotte.

The What Ifs

Sarah Coles was nervously waiting for the return of her daughter. She hadn't heard from Jim, so had no idea what was happening or if the men had found any more clues. Her daughter was a strong woman. Whatever happened to her, Sarah was sure Charlotte had survived it. She had plenty of time to think of all of things she and Jim had been through raising their daughter. Even though Charlotte was an adult on her own, she thought about how she had discouraged Charlotte from seeing Seth, but Charlotte charged on anyway. It ended up being a great relationship to Sarah's surprise. Her daughter was right about how editing in the news can frame people differently from who they really are. Sarah had always thought of him as too rough for her daughter. She had made that judgement based on the many news clips she had seen. Now Sarah saw Seth as a courageous, thoughtful person not some wild man like she had always pictured in the past.

Doubt was creeping into Sarah's mind as the wait seemed endless to hear some news. What if we never find her then what do we do, she thought. What if Charlotte is holding on as hard as she can and gives up? No, Charlotte wouldn't do that. What if she's wandering around somewhere and doesn't know who she is? What if we never see her again? I don't think I can do that, Sarah thought. I know I can't do that. All of these thoughts were swirling around in her mind. Time was moving so slowly. I'm not going to give up. It won't be long now. Jim will call to tell me they found her, she thought.

Sarah's phone began vibrating. It was sitting on the wooden table next to her. She was elated to see that it was Jim. Sarah picked up the phone without saying hello. Her first words were, "Tell me you found her Jim."

Jim's voice was choppy on Sarah's end. All she could make out was, "Charl and cree"

Sarah yelled into the phone, "Jim, you're breaking up. I can't make out what you're saying." Then Sarah heard this loud screeching sound over the phone. It sounded like metal scraping against metal. She could hear the wind too, but couldn't hear anything Jim was saying. It was still broken pieces of words that made no sense. Sarah yelled into the phone, "The connection is bad Jim. Call me back later." It was so disappointing not to be able to understand what was going on. Sarah put her phone back on the table. She slumped into her rocking chair rocking slowly, "Dear Lord, I'm trying so hard to be patient. Please give me the strength I need. Thank you Lord. In Jesus' name, Amen."

It's Cloaked

Jim was looking up to the sky as he dropped his phone not knowing what he was hearing. Seth, Nicholas, David, and Lucy were all looking up to the sky as well. A strong breeze had kicked up enough to make the water splash around in the creek. There was a sound above them that sounded like metal scraping against metal. Lucy cowered behind Jim. Scott was busy with Charlotte. He had put a portable compressor on her chest. It was doing deep compressions to get her heart started again.

Suddenly the strange noises from the sky stopped. Lucy came out from behind Jim. David looked to the other men, "There was nothing in the sky."

Seth agreed, "The sky was clear. It was cloaked!"

Nicholas agreed, "Either that thing was cloaked or we're fall down drunk."

Scott was still keeping an eye on Charlotte, "No time to think about that. Somebody needs to get us a medic chopper and NOW!"

David and Lucy jumped to attention, "We're on that. We'll head back to call a chopper." David and his dog began running as fast as they could back to the vehicles to contact the chopper.

David yelled back at the group, "Don't worry, they'll be here fast!"

Seth looked at Scott, "Is she going to make it?"

Scott nodded, "I got this."